P9-AOD-806

The Malcontent

THE NEW MERMAIDS

General Editors
PHILIP BROCKBANK
BRIAN MORRIS

The Malcontent

JOHN MARSTON

Edited by BERNARD HARRIS

A New Mermaid

A MERMAID DRAMABOOK

HILL AND WANG • NEW YORK

©*Ernest Benn Limited 1967*
All rights reserved
Standard Book Number (paperback edition): 8090-1112-3
Standard Book Number (clothbound edition): 8090-6715-3
Library of Congress catalog card number: 69-16836

First American Edition May 1969

Manufactured in the United States of America

1234567890

IN MEMORY
OF
CHARLES J. SISSON

CONTENTS

ACKNOWLEDGEMENTS

FOR BIOGRAPHICAL AUTHORITY and certain relevant commentary I have relied on Arnold Davenport's *The Poems of John Marston* (1961).

Among editions of Marston's plays I have made most use of the collected works edited by A. H. Bullen (1887) and H. A. Wood (1934), and the texts of *The Malcontent* edited by W. A. Neilson (1911), G. B. Harrison (1933), C. F. Tucker Brooke and N. B. Paradise (1933), R. G. Lawrence (1963), R. C. Harrier (1963) and M. L. Wine (1964). For commentary on the Induction I remain indebted to F. L. Lucas, *The Complete Works of John Webster* (1927), Vol. III. Where specifically cited these editions are referred to by their editors' surnames.

The present text has been prepared with the assistance of books and microfilms, for the use of which I have to thank the Directors of the British Museum, the Folger Shakespeare Library, and the Shakespeare Institute (University of Birmingham). I am further indebted to the Librarians of Leeds University and York University.

I wish to thank Professor G. K. Hunter for the benefits of conversation and correspondence; Mr Leo Salingar for further suggestions; Dr. Brian Gibbons and the General Editors for cognitive and cogitative discussions.

BERNARD HARRIS

York 1967

INTRODUCTION

THE AUTHOR

JOHN MARSTON was baptised on 7 October 1576 at Wardington, Oxfordshire, where his parents—John Marston, Reader of the Middle Temple, and Marie Guarsi, daughter of an Italian surgeon—had been married on 19 September 1575. He matriculated at Brasenose College, Oxford in 1592, became a member of the Middle Temple in the same year, and graduated B.A. at Oxford in 1594. His father died in 1599, willing his law-books to his son, but acknowledging that 'man proposeth and God disposeth'; and though Marston occupied chambers from 1595 to 1606 he studied philosophy rather than law, and made his career in letters and religion.

Marston's first published work, *The Metamorphosis of Pigmalions Image and Certaine Satyres* (1598), contained an erotic Ovidian poem and five satires, in one of which Joseph Hall was attacked. The tone and intention of the title-poem, and the occasion of the attempted forced quarrel with a fellow satirist, have been frequently yet inconclusively explored. Whether from true grievance, imagined hurt or calculated publicity the running references were sustained in Marston's more substantial contribution to Elizabethan satire, *The Scourge of Villanie* (1598), which was dedicated to 'his best beloved Selfe', offered next to the spirit of 'Detraction', and consigned in an epilogue to 'Everlasting Oblivion'. The ten satires of this collection ('Lashing the lewdnesse of Britannia') were augmented in the second edition of 1599 by 'Satyra Nova'—a fresh challenge to Hall—and the book reached a third edition in that year before the Bishops' Ban of June 1599 brought a number of scurrilous, licentious or allegedly subversive pamphlets, poems and histories to a bonfire in the yard of Stationers' Hall.

Before the proscription upon satires, however, Marston had turned dramatist, probably beginning by revising such old plays as *Histriomastix* and *Jack Drum's Entertainment* for Paul's Boys, and before long he was 'managing his paper pen-knife gallantly' in the War of the Theatres. If the quarrel with Hall was literary pretence, Marston's battle with Ben Jonson seems to have had more artistic pretentiousness: it was a war of words in which Marston's 'ruffian style'—as the *Parnassus* poets termed it—served well enough until Jonson devised his unanswerable *Poetaster*. With *Antonio and Mellida* and *Antonio's Revenge* (probably acted in 1599), however, Marston's claims as a serious and original poetic dramatist were as evident as his satiric skills.

In 1601 Marston, Shakespeare, Jonson and Chapman were described as the 'best and chiefest of our modern writers' when they added their poems to Robert Chester's *Love's Martyr*. Yet Marston's literary career was over before the end of the decade. He wrote *What You Will* (probably performed in 1601) as a final participation in the War of the Theatres. *The Dutch Courtesan* (probably acted in 1603–4), and later plays, were written for the Queen's Revels boys' company acting in Blackfriars: by the time of *The Malcontent* (probably composed in 1604), acted first by the boys and later by the King's Men at the Globe, Marston had settled his differences with Ben Jonson and dedicated the play to him. In 1605 the two dramatists collaborated with Chapman in the comedy of *Eastward Ho!*, for which Chapman and Jonson, and probably all three men, were imprisoned. Marston wrote a commendatory verse for Jonson's *Sejanus* (printed 1605), but their enmity seems to have revived, and references in the prefatory material of Marston's next two plays appear to be critical of Jonson. Indeed, after writing *Parasitaster or The Fawne* (1605) and *Sophonisba* (1606) Marston's interest in the theatre generally seems to have diminished. He was in the country in the summer of 1607 when he wrote his *Entertainment of the Dowager Countess of Derby* for the Huntingdon family at Ashby de la Zouch. In June 1608 the Privy Council committed him to Newgate, for unknown cause and period. His last play, *The Insatiate Countess*, probably written in the same year, is believed to have been left unfinished, and to have been completed by William Barksted in 1610.

On 24 September 1609 Marston had been ordained Deacon at Stanton Harcourt in Oxfordshire, by John Bridges, Bishop of Oxford, and on 24 December 1609 Marston was ordained priest. When and where Marston married Mary Wilkes is uncertain. She was the daughter of Dr William Wilkes, incumbent of Barford, Wiltshire and a chaplain to James I: when Wilkes died in 1630 he left Marston a gold ring, inscribed with the Guarsi arms, and forgave him a debt incurred by eleven years of lodging 'with his wife, his man and his maid'. Davenport points out that since Marston became incumbent of Christchurch, Hampshire on 10 October 1616 the eleven years presumably ended then, suggesting that Marston was married in 1605. Marston's life with his in-laws gave an opportunity to Ben Jonson for his observation to Drummond that 'Marston wrott his Father jn Lawes preachings & his Father jn Law his Commedies'.

Marston's only son died in 1624, in infancy. On 13 September

1631 Marston resigned the living of Christchurch. He made his will on 17 June 1634, leaving £77 in bequests to relatives and to parishioners of Christchurch, his silver basin and ewer to Richard Marston, cousin, of New Inn, and the residue of his estate, with loving phrases, to his wife. Marston died on 25 June 1634 at his house in Aldermanbury, London, and was buried next day beside his father in the Choir of the Temple Church. Mary Marston died in 1657, and was buried with her husband, sharing the tombstone epitaph which evoked his early intentions to be a scourger of villainy and was descriptive of his final hopes, 'Oblivioni Sacrum'.

THE PLAY

I. DATE AND OCCASION

'An Enterlude called the Male-content, Tragicomoedia' was entered on the Stationers' Register on 5 July 1604 to William Aspley and Thomas Thorpe. Three editions were printed by Valentine Simmes within that same year. The relationship between these editions is briefly summarised in the Note on the Text.

The theatrical occasion of the play is as complex a problem as that of the transmission of the text, since these matters are mutually dependent. The third impression of *The Malcontent* contains extensive additional material, together with John Webster's Induction to the play. In this, leading actors of the King's Men discuss the play's acquisition, the reason for the additional material, and the dramatist's intentions:

SLY
  I would know how you came by this play.
CONDELL
  Faith, sir, the book was lost, and because 'twas pity so good a play should be lost, we found it and play it.
SLY
  I wonder you would play it, another company having interest in it.
CONDELL
  Why not Malevole in folio with us, as Jeronimo in decimo-sexto with them? They taught us a name for our play, we call it *One for another*.
SLY
  What are your additions?
BURBAGE
  Sooth, not greatly needful, only as your sallet to your great feast, to entertain a little more time, and to abridge the not-received custom of music in our theatre.

Scholars have shared Sly's thoughts and have enlarged upon the answers he received until a fairly satisfactory hypothesis of the play's history has emerged. This presumes that Marston wrote the first version of *The Malcontent* for performance by the Children of the Queen's Revels (Hamlet's 'little eyasses') at Blackfriars. The book of the play was then lost, either truly or feignedly so, and the King's Men acquired it as a move in the War of the Theatres, so retaliating for the Children's performance of a King's Men play, *The First Part of Jeronimo*, usually dated 1600–2.

Being choristers the Children naturally made full use of their musical talents in theatrical presentation, as F. L. Lucas notes. The adult companies, about this period, were developing an interest in theatre music, and Jonson's *Sejanus* had been performed at the Globe theatre in 1603 with music between the acts. But Burbage's remark about the 'not-received custom' remains evidence for current practice, and it seems probable that the first version of *The Malcontent* contained too much music for the taste of the Globe audience, and possibly for the resources of the King's Men. Accordingly, Marston contributed additional material, and Webster furnished the play with an induction which followed the example of Jonson's *Every Man Out Of His Humour* (printed 1600) in putting the induction to critical use, and, of course, served the ends of publicity. The joke about 'folio' and 'decimo-sexto' draws plainly upon the rivalry of child and adult players. Hence, Marston's dedication of the play to Jonson may be seen as both a gesture of personal reconciliation and an act of re-dedication of his own art.

Such an hypothesis does not explain all the circumstances of the play's occasion. We do not know when the original version of *The Malcontent* was written. Older commentators were content to cite the allusion at I. viii, 19, calculating from it a date of 1600: but Sir E. K. Chambers can provide no evidence for Marston's association with the Children of the Queen's Revels before 1604. Again, we cannot be sure that the additional material is wholly Marston's. E. E. Stoll argued on stylistic grounds for the presence of Webster's hand, but though F. L. Lucas confirms that some passages are 'sometimes exceedingly like Webster's later work' he also reminds us of the deep influence Marston had upon Webster. Nor can we say confidently what proportion of the additional material may consist of restored copy, or revision. What seems apparent from the nature of some topical references is that the augmented text of *The Malcontent* was not completed until 1604.

That the play should have been pressed into service in the War of the Theatres is a puzzling and probably only tangential fact. But Marston had been so heavily committed in the affair that no work of his at this period could escape involvement. We may presume that Webster was required to write an induction, even though Marston had displayed an original aptitude for this activity in *Antonio and Mellida*, in order to give colourable circumstance to the account of the play's theft.

The attraction which *The Malcontent* held for the King's Men may be suggested both in terms of commercial value and of theatrical art. The vogue for satiric drama was at its height, and Marston is here at his most pointed and formidable. From his comments in the preface 'To the reader' about those persons who 'have been most unadvisedly over-cunning in misinterpreting' the author's intentions, and have 'maliciously spread ill rumours' it seems likely that *The Malcontent* had either drawn readily speculative glances, or that they are being provocatively invited. The play seems comparatively free from the kind of personal allusion exchanged in works directly engaged in the War of the Theatres, but its references to corrupt practices in religion and to dishonest policy were undoubtedly the subject of some revision.

More immediately compelling, however, than the play's outspokenness upon such topics as court immorality and intrigues for power, so much canvassed in the contemporary satiric drama, may have been the generous opportunities afforded by *The Malcontent* for the full employment of stage conventions, in terms of character, role and disguise, transitions of speech and action, and ironic manipulations of tone and viewpoint. To some extent *The Malcontent* is a play for an actors' theatre, of gratifying interest initially to such a company as the King's Men, practised in the diverse modes of *Every Man Out Of His Humour* and *Hamlet*. The Induction tells us that Richard Burbage played Malevole, a sustained duple-role suited to the actor who had performed Richard III, Hamlet, almost certainly Macilente, and who would create Webster's Ferdinand. Henry Condell, the future Cardinal of *The Duchess of Malfi*, may have taken Duke Pietro, though, if Baldwin is right in assigning to him Horatio, the loyal confidant Celso is an obvious possibility. John Lowin, whose parts included comedians and heavy villains, seems a natural Mendoza. William Sly, for whom an Admiral's Men inventory of 1598 mentions a 'Perowes sewt', might have been Bilioso; and John Sinklo, for whom we have some indication of comic roles, may have been an appropriate Passarello.

Such attributions, Malevole apart, are merely fanciful, but they are intended as reminders that *The Malcontent* once held a place in the repertory of the most talented company of the day. Indeed, some understanding of the play's immediate theatrical environment is a necessary prerequisite for useful criticism of a work which has long

lost its audience, seems unlikely to regain one, and yet which continues to demand from its readers an attentiveness to dramatic and
theatrical presentation.

The Malcontent is a theatrically ambitious and bewilderingly
active play, rich in details of staging. It requires the formality of
court drama, calling for attendants, pages, lights, ladies, processions,
music, dancing and the devising of a masque: it makes theatrical
points with costume and jewellery, the preparation of food and the
customs of the chase. It fully exploits and exhibits disguises of
person and deceits of mind, discoveries of identity and reversals of
disposition. Its language shifts from philosophic reflection to bawdy
abuse, from pathetic description and virtuous sentiment to serious
invective.

That double-response to the presentation of character and action
which the stage conventions elicited and the mode of tragi-comedy
required can be properly achieved only by the discipline of staging;
without it a reader is often conscious of contradiction, irrelevance
and repetition, where a theatre-goer would experience ironic reversal,
sequential underscoring and dramatic emphasis. The music to *The
Malcontent* has not survived, and with it has been lost a necessary
element in the process of preparing, adjusting, or 'keying' audience-
response.

There remain some severe barriers to our understanding of the
successful presentation of the play, and Marston himself must take
some blame for allowing himself or others to disturb the original
pattern of his play by processes of accretion. Nor can we reasonably
claim, from the nature of Marston's other writings, that his habitual
obscurity has been more than superficially extended by poor printing
and negligent punctuation.

But however unsatisfactory it is to defend *The Malcontent* as a
work of dramatic art by appealing to a theatre of judgement in which
it is unlikely now to be tried, it would be conspicuously unwise, in
turning to critical consideration of the play, to ignore the truth
within the commonplace several times repeated by Marston and
here offered 'To the reader':

> only one thing afflicts me, to think that scenes invented merely to be
> spoken should be enforcively published to be read.

2. STORY AND STRUCTURE

The narrative basis of *The Malcontent* seems worth recounting so
that its relationship with other literary forms, in the absence of an
established source, may become clearer.

Giovanni Altofronto, Duke of Genoa, but deprived of power by

Pietro Jacomo, continues to live at the usurper's court disguised as Malevole the malcontent, and known only to his friend Celso.

Pietro's wife, Aurelia, commits adultery with Mendoza, one of Pietro's faction. Malevole reveals the fact to Pietro. But Aurelia, tricked by Maquerelle the bawd, discards Mendoza and takes Ferneze as her lover. Mendoza convinces Pietro of his innocence, and is made Pietro's heir. Together they plan to surprise Ferneze and kill him, but in such a manner that Mendoza will seem to be Ferneze's defender, so securing Aurelia's favour again and ensuring that Mendoza will become her confidant should she attempt to revenge herself upon Pietro. The plot works, though Ferneze recovers in secret and joins with Malevole and Celso.

Mendoza, acting for Aurelia and himself, bribes Malevole to kill Pietro while hunting. It is agreed that Malevole shall throw Pietro's body in the sea and falsely report that Pietro has committed suicide in distraction at Aurelia's disgrace.

Malevole reveals the plot to Pietro, who disguises himself as a hermit, returns to the court, and gives circumstantial description of his own death. Mendoza seizes the opportunity to banish Aurelia, and then sends Malevole to fetch from imprisonment his own duchess, Maria, whom Mendoza proposes to marry for reasons of political security. Further, having inherited Pietro's dukedom, Mendoza seeks to strengthen his power; he schemes to destroy both Malevole and the hermit (Pietro) by arranging that they shall poison each other in the citadel. The place is chosen to implicate Maria and so compel her through fear into marriage with Mendoza.

The cumulative logic of such resourceful villainy causes Pietro to repent of his own earlier treachery, and he declares his intention of seeking the restoration of Duke Altofronto. Malevole accordingly reveals his true identity. He tricks Mendoza into believing both in the hermit's death and in the certainty that Malevole has been poisoned.

At the masque which the triumphant Mendoza arranges for Maria's return, Malevole, Pietro, Celso and Ferneze appear as four Genoan dukes. Malevole and Pietro are re-united with their wives during the dance. Then the disguises are abandoned, Altofronto is restored by acclaim, and Mendoza is banished.

The story has no known source, and Marston declares in his preface to the reader that 'in some things I have willingly erred, as in supposing a Duke of Genoa, and in taking names different from that city's families'. These matters must be discussed later in the context of literary themes and their presentation; what follows here are some observations upon Marston's dramatic handling of his story.

One of the pleasures of *The Malcontent* lies in the speed and flexibility of Marston's development of the predictable surprises of his plot. He refrains from complicating the action with a sub-plot, though he provides contrast, caricature and incidental satire in the subsidiary characters and the activities of court servants. In an attempt to preserve the effectiveness of scene-transitions Marston's original scene-division has been retained in this edition; to tidy them up in the manner of most modernising editions is to inflict additional footnotes upon a reader without any particular benefit. But it must be conceded that the additions found in the third edition necessarily hinder the relatively simpler, and possibly more effective, dramatic action of the original version. These additional passages have been listed in the Note on the Text, and this edition does not draw attention to them upon the page. The main passages, however, require comment in terms of the play's final structure.

In I. iii Marston inserted a forty-line speech by Malevole of a nature calculated to increase Pietro's misery at the news of his wife's adultery and to spur him to revenge; at the end of the scene Malevole is given a soliloquy of seventeen lines.

In I. iv Bilioso, the court marshal, enters and interrupts an existing scene between Malevole and Celso to the extent of some forty-three lines.

I. viii is an additional scene between Malevole and Passarello, the latter being a new character found only in the augmented version.

V. i begins with an additional exchange between Bilioso and Passarello, his fool, for fifty-one lines; these lead into the original opening for the scene, which further contains an inserted exchange, involving Passarello again, at lines 61–87.

In V. ii some thirty lines have been added to the end of the scene to provide a further entrance for Bilioso.

In V. iii the existing texts preserve both the original scene between Malevole and Mendoza and additional matter amounting to some fourteen lines intended in part to cancel some of the retained original text.

In V. iv Malevole's penultimate speech has been extended by a dozen lines or so, followed by two comments from Maquerelle and Bilioso.

It is perhaps hazardous to write of an 'original version' of *The Malcontent*, since it is possible that part of these additions represent restored readings, similar to those found in other, more minor discrepancies, between the augmented impression and the earlier impressions. However, it is noticeable that these major additions occur in either the first act or the last, where they could most easily extend the length of the less musical version without undue dis-location of the strongly plotted main structure.

Obviously these additions were undertaken for theatrical expedi-
ency, but it is worth emphasising Marston's dramatic tact when
engaged in augmenting his play. The nature of the majority of the
additions might suggest mere padding and explicit indulgence in
buffoonery. Seven of the ten major additional passages are prose, all
devoted to building up the character of Bilioso and giving life to his
fool. Yet they are neither the most grievous examples of Jacobean
comic scenes, nor is Passarello the most negligible clown. The scenes
sharpen the criticism of court manners and modes of entertainment;
the choice of Bilioso as ambassador is made more ridiculous; the
theme of parasitic and merely politic friendship is more fully presented; and some funny stories are recounted by the way. Of the
three serious verse passages, that in which Malevole incites Pietro,
and that in which Malevole reflects upon Mendoza's treachery,
perhaps involve some loss of dramatic tension; but Malevole's
additional soliloquy is one of the major dramatic benefits of the play.

It seems clear then that Marston had no alternative in adapting
the play for the capacities of the King's Men than to extend the
playing time by providing more opportunity for comic playing as a
substitute for the inherent element of caricature afforded by the use
of boy players in the serious roles. The reduction of the music must
have entailed a loss of dramatic efficiency which Marston hoped to
minimise by apportioning his additional material to balance his
central concerns.

Yet it would be false to imply that Marston abandoned a highly
developed dramatic structure and connived in its trivialisation for
use by the adult players. For it is apparent that Marston's notion
of what constituted a dramatic structure always depended upon the
disconcerting and deliberately disjunctive contrivances of tragi-
comedy. Speech and style, character and role, are adjusted and
manipulated with much of the intention, and some of the means,
that Marston used in his verse satires. There, savage depiction,
incoherent utterance, and imperfect vision are not deficiencies
explicable only by reference to poetic theory, but energies being
released into poetic and moral consciousness. The same point may
be made about Marston's drama. Criticism that is preoccupied with
the quarrels of the satirists and the War of the Theatres tends to see
rivalry of styles, burlesque and direct allusion more in terms of the
competing writers and less as experiments and achievements within
the exploitable possibilities of dramatic forms. Some recent critics,
however, have justly compared present-day experience of theatrical
experiment in explaining their response to Marston. Thus, M. L.
Wine adapts a line from Genet's *The Blacks* in suggesting the kind
of distance between audience and art that would be accomplished by

child actors.[1] And G. K. Hunter, defending the 'clash of opposites' in *Antonio and Mellida* as productive of more than comedy, observes that 'A modern play like *Waiting for Godot* should remind us that the tragic and the absurd may belong together'; indeed Hunter sees 'a characteristic ambivalence of outlook which makes Marston one of the strangest as well as one of the most modern of the Elizabethans'.[2]

Such comments help us to realise that *The Malcontent* escapes the categories of historical dramatic definition not through its author's carelessness or indifference but through artistic necessity; it breaks all the moulds it has assembled, discards all the masks it has assumed, and this extravagant mode of behaviour, sensationally 'theatrical', is revelatory of its main dramatic procedures, which expose a major crime, attended on by a multitude of lesser villainies, and reveal a major virtue, dissimulated on a score of occasions until persistent human enterprise enables it to walk naked.

3. THEMES AND PRESENTATION

Several contexts, literary and dramatic, to which *The Malcontent* can be referred, may have value if such contexts are understood not as limits for the play's art but as suggestions about the nature of some of its concerns.

The Malcontent, by attention to themes of corrupt state-craft, and by use of Senecal stage conventions, is related to plays loosely ascribed to the 'revenge tradition'. Its philosophical 'sentences', passionate speeches and ritual movement in dance and masque remind us of *The Spanish Tragedy* and anticipate *The Revenger's Tragedy*. *Hamlet* is echoed, and its special qualities of self-disgust, corrupted sensibility and moral fortitude remain influential. Yet *The Malcontent* contains no actual murder, though several are intended; and its hero exacts no vengeance, though the movement of the action appears designed to accomplish an act of fearful retribution. The satirical element so complements the tragic that R. C. Harrier has placed *The Malcontent* along with *Every Man in His Humour*, *The White Devil* and *Bussy D'Ambois* to 'exemplify the close relation of satire and tragedy notable towards the end of Elizabeth's reign and the beginning of James I's'.[3] Yet although Malevole displays certain attitudes already exhibited by some of Jonson's characters, and later to be developed in Webster's creations, the special malcontentedness

---

[1] *The Malcontent*, ed. M. L. Wine, 1964, p. xxv.
[2] *Antonio and Mellida*, ed. G. K. Hunter, 1965, p. xvii.
[3] *An Anthology of Jacobean Drama*, Vol. I, ed. R. C. Harrier, New York University Press, 1963, p. vii.

of Marston's world lacks the intellectual clarity of Jonson's comedy and the sense of inevitability present in Webster's tragedies. A. Caputi observes that 'evil in *The Malcontent* is largely an atmosphere, an atmosphere appropriate to the didactic and satiric burdens of the play, and at the same time appropriate to the comic resolution'.[1] Perhaps the only Jacobean play which provides some of that atmosphere, outside Marston's own work, is Webster's *The Devil's Law-Case*, which sometimes recalls the defunctive note of Marston's grotesque rhetoric.

Yet if *The Malcontent* makes neither a substantial contribution to the notion of a 'revenge tradition', nor creates a convincing influence of its own, it possesses important associations with certain plays of its own immediate period, distinct in kind but connected by major themes and the activity of their central characters. Writing of Vindice in *The Revenger's Tragedy*, and his status as 'avenger, satirist and tempter', L. G. Salingar notes that 'There are close analogies to his role and his speeches in *Hamlet*, *The Malcontent*, *The Fawn*, *Volpone*, and Middleton's comedies assignable to the years shortly before 1606.'[2] To this list can obviously be added works specifically centred upon the figure of the prince in disguise; thus, to Marston's *Malcontent* and *Fawn*, and Middleton's *Phoenix*, Hunter adds Sharpham's *Fleer*, Day's *Law Tricks* and Shakespeare's *Measure for Measure*.[3] The presence of didactic comedy in such lists is sufficient to indicate that serious matters of traditional moral reproof might, under satirical scrutiny, yield to optimistic design.

The confusion of genres is made complete, perhaps, by Condell's assertion (in the Induction) that *The Malcontent* is a history. The play is of course a feigned history whose origins lie as much in Marston's earlier work as in any true reports of Italy. In *Antonio and Mellida* the disinherited Antonio, heir to another Duke of Genoa, stays on at the court from which he has been banished, and adopts the protective role of a fool. He refrains from the alternative possibility of becoming 'a spitting critic'. By adopting precisely this form of disguise, as the cynic Malevole, Giovanni Altofronto, deposed Duke of Genoa, remains an active figure at the centre of the world from which he has been excluded. He is thus the ideal agent for the introduction of Marston's existing modes of satire into dramatic form, and for the demonstration of the social effectiveness of the satiric outlook. For only by combining within one such dominant

---

[1] A. Caputi, *John Marston, Satirist*, Cornell University Press, 1961, p. 186.
[2] L. G. Salingar, '*The Revenger's Tragedy*: some possible sources', *MLR*, LX, 1965, 11.
[3] G. K. Hunter, 'English Folly and Italian Vice', in *Jacobean Theatre* (*Stratford-upon-Avon Studies*, 1), 1960, p. 101, n. 19.

character the source of authority, the capacity to test it, and the means of dramatic duplicity in regaining it, could Marston achieve that final reconciliation between private and public interests which is essential for the comic outcome.

Marston does not exploit the possibilities of the literal feigned history, so that the political relationships of the Genoese and Florentines are touched on vaguely, and the business of the embassy of Bilioso is built up for no final purpose. Yet the reasons for removing his satiric gaze from metropolitan citizenry to the world of Renaissance courts were more complex than the obviously expedient necessity to study political corruption within a framework other than that provided in England. G. K. Hunter has demonstrated that 'the Guicciardini period of Italian history was well known to the Jacobeans as a *corpus vile* for political dissections by the new scientific methods', and also that Marston had 'discovered in the world of Guicciardini's Italy a natural background for the self-torturing individualism of the Malcontent observer, who saw that the atmosphere of corrupted power could be crystallised by setting a solitary, cynical 'observer' against a procession of sophisticated and self-confident vice'.[1]

I.   I. ii, 6

Marston's choice of some characters' names from Florio's *A Worlde of Wordes* (1598) hints at the possibility that this paraded life might be typified in the fashion of the morality tradition and Marston's own early practice. Thus Malevole's true designation of 'Altofronto' means 'high forehead'; his loyal friend 'Celso' may be understood as 'high', 'noble' or 'bright'; Mendoza, as 'Mendoso', suggests 'faultie, that may be mended'. Some names seem uncharacteristic, as 'Bilioso', or merely descriptive of function, as 'Prepasso' the usher; it is possible that Ferrardo owes his name to 'Ferrare',

[1] *Loc. cit.*, pp. 102–3.

which can mean 'to tagge points', and that Guerrino is so-called because he is referred to as a prisoner. Certainly the most important of the court servants is Maquerelle; 'Macarello' offers 'a baude or a pander', as well as 'mackrel' and 'a rauenous fowle'. It is clear how we take Maquerelle, but possible that the other associations lead to 'passerelle' as 'flounders' or as 'dride fish called poore Iohn', and to 'Bianchetto', as 'Bianca', variously meaning 'prettie and white', 'a Dace' or 'a Menow'.

This kind of nomenclature is suggestive, however, and not mechanical. Some figures, Pietro Jacomo, Aurelia, Maria, and Ferneze, seem excluded from the process, which is never obtrusive. Indeed, a play which deals so much with themes of deception, self-deception and dissimulation could scarcely afford a consistency of character definition. The use to which Marston puts the names of his actual characters is perhaps only part of a larger activity involving the creation of further inhabited worlds seen as extensions of the play-world. The largest of these categories of additional names derives from classical literature; another is spun out of figures of Arthurian and chivalric romance; a third consists of contemporary invention, like Doctor Plaster-face, Sir Oliver Anchovy, or Count Quidlibet-in-Quodlibet. Such displays of names assist the bewildering change of tone, direction of attention, and point of allusion

II.   II. iii, 17–22

customary in satiric reflection; but the intention is more than to
widen the range of the audience's perception, it is also a means of
insistent focus. For the names which spring readily to Malevole's
lips throughout this play are associated with notions of sexual
appetite (Ganymede, Hercules, Ixion, who begat centaurs upon
clouds—an activity peculiarly consonant with Marston's phantas-
magorical impression), with the cuckolded victims of this desire
(Agamemnon, Menelaus or King Arthur), or with partners in sexual
offence (Paris and Helen, Aegisthus and Clytemnestra, Lancelot and
Guinevere). Specifically, of course, most of these names are associated with the theme of adultery, and are thereby related to the
theme of the essential action of the play, that of usurpation and its
attendant topics of treachery and inconstancy.

III.   I. ii, 14–15

The intimate connection, no less than in *Hamlet*, between private
and public acts, is established at the beginning of *The Malcontent*,
when Malevole begins his long and devious struggle to regain his
dukedom by informing Pietro of his wife's adultery with Mendoza.
Thus, one form of usurpation becomes the means by which Malevole
provokes successive acts of usurpation, turning a wheel which brings
him round eventually to his own rightful position.

In re-affirming the relationships between political behaviour and
personal morality Marston relies heavily upon continuous declara-
tions of sententious opinion, but prevents these from burdening the

IV. IV. iii, 37–8

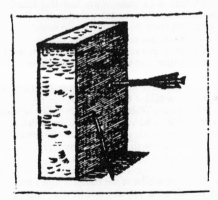

V. II. iii, 58–9

play with inept platitudes by frequent surprises of characters' natures and the consequences of action. Thus, Pietro, the original aggressor, becomes a penitent; Mendoza, initially presented as a sensual opportunist, becomes a major villain. The sources of some sententious opinions are often emblematic.

One example of Marston's ability to utilise material, different in nature and emphasis, to reinforce his particular concerns, lies in his manipulation of Guarini's *Il pastor fido*. Marston, as G. K. Hunter observes, had been 'reading up this prototype of tragi-comedy while preparing his own *aspera Thalia*', but his borrowings show skilful employment rather than easy plunder. The longest passage used reveals the most complex handling: it is taken from the 1602 translation of *Il pastor fido* (III. v), from a discussion in which Corisca, the wanton nymph, tests the attitude of Amarillis, the heroine, towards honour:

CORISCA
This honestie is but an art to seeme so,
Let others as they list beleeue, Ile think so still.
AMARILLIS
These are but vanities (Corisca) t'were best
Quickly to leaue that which we cannot hold.
CORISCA
And who forbids thee foole? This life's too short
To passe it ouer with one onely loue:
Men are too sparing of their fauors now,
(Whether't be for want, or else for frowardnesse)
The fresher that we are, the dearer still:
Beautie and youth once gone w'are like Bee hiues
That hath no honey, no nor yet no waxe.
Let men prate on they do not feele our woes,
For their condition differs much from ours,
The elder that they grow, they grow the perfecter:
If they loose beautie, yet they wisedome gaine:
But when our beautie fades that oftentimes
Conquers their greatest witts, strait fadeth all our good,
There cannot be a vilder thing to see
Then an old woman. Therefore ere thou age attaine,
Know me thy selfe, and vse it as thou shouldst.
What were a Lion worth did he not vse his strength?
What's a man's wit worth that lies idly by?
Eu'n so our beautie proper strength to vs,
As force to Lyons, wisedome vnto men,
We ought to vse it whilst it we haue. Time flies
Away and yeares come on, our youth once lost
We like cut flowres neuer grow fresh againe.
And to our hoary haires loue well may runne,
But Louers will our wrinkled skinnes still shunne.[1]

Some of the phrasing, and much of the sentiment, of Corisca's traditional advice is put, appropriately enough, into the mouth of Maquerelle, as part of her instructions to the court ladies, Bianca

---

[1] *Il Pastor Fido: or the Faithful Shepherd. Translated out of Italian into English.* London. Printed for Simon Waterson. 1602. Sig. H4r-v. See *The Malcontent*, II. iv. Some other borrowings are indicated in the notes to the text.

and Emilia, in II. iv. The placing of this scene, however, increases the dramatic, as well as the literary, propriety of Marston's use of Guarini. In the preceding scene Pietro and Mendoza have plotted to surprise Aurelia and Ferneze, and destroy Ferneze: in the succeeding scene Mendoza enters and waits outside the door of Aurelia's bedroom, with drawn sword, ready to kill Ferneze. Maquerelle's speech, therefore, occupies the time between the declaration of murderous intent and the execution of the deed. So that while Aurelia and Ferneze commit adultery, Maquerelle advises the younger court bawds in the preparation of a posset; but the eloquence of her defence is addressed to us as much as to them; our feelings are reorganised just as much as theirs are incited. The elegiac quality in the nymph's exhortation, its appeal to our sense of transient youth, decayed beauty and diminished passion, is made more poignant by being put into the mouth of the aged Maquerelle. Moreover, the sentiments have further relevance to the situation being enacted but not presented. Aurelia's penitence, later in the play, proves the more acceptable, perhaps, because of this scene, which ends with Maquerelle's prayer for the success of this 'posset's operation' upon the disposition of the court ladies. Our feelings are worked upon; Maquerelle, in fact, is the true bawd.

The next scene, too, is an example of the play's purposive handling of reversals of mood, opinion and characters' sentiments. Mendoza's treachery, in trying to kill Ferneze while seeming to save him, is a piece of successful duplicity which temporarily restores him to Aurelia's confidence, and simultaneously permits him to retain Pietro's favour. This episode in Mendoza's scheme to gain political power by means of the double deceit practised upon a ruler and his wife seems reminiscent of a moment in the pre-history of Giraldi's *Selene*. There the villain, Gripo, secretary to the Queen, informs King Rodobano, falsely, of his wife's infidelity, arranges an ambush in which he intends to kill the King, and turns his subsequent failure to do so into an advantage by pretending that he has saved the Queen from her husband's assault.

The point that needs to be made here is not the local and specific one of a source for an episode, but the more general one of typical figures, representative themes and similarity of ideals. For Marston reminds one more closely of Giraldi than of any English contemporary dramatist in his treatment of tyranny and infidelity. On these topics Giraldi's most persuasive critic has written that:

It was compassion rather than terror that he wanted his audience to feel, for it was with the experience of compassion that he identified the secret pleasure latent in the tragic spectacle. This conception, so far from suggesting a morbid mentality, was part and parcel of a general outlook conditioned by the humanistic culture in which the writer grew up.[1]

Furthermore, associated with the theme of tyranny and infidelity

are two ideal figures, the function of which is to affirm the value of the ideals of clemency and fidelity, particularly fidelity to the marriage vow. They are the figure of the just and clement ruler (typified by the emperor in *Epitia*) and the figure of the faithful wife (as represented by the heroines of *Euphemia* and *Arrenopia*).

The relationship between *Epitia* and *Measure for Measure* has long been proposed, and it seems worth while to emphasise how much *The Malcontent* shares the 'idealistic content' of Giraldi's tragedies. Attention to this thematic material furnishes a defence against critics who have argued, in J. Peter's terms, that 'the structure of the play is defective, and so is the conception of its chief character, Malevole'.[2] Disappointment here is with 'the play's building up to a consummation that never really comes', for 'The whole drift of the play leads on towards some kind of retribution for Mendoza's villainy', and 'Yet when it comes to the point, with Mendoza pleading for his life, Malevole merely reproves . . . and dismisses him as a fly'. Peter's explanation of this shortcoming is that Marston erred in *Antonio's Revenge*, where he had 'indeed pursued his theme to its logical conclusion, with the revengers' execution of Piero, but he had done it in a way that went far to vitiate the tragedy'. He recognised the flaw 'and over-corrected for it in *The Malcontent*, by making his second set of revengers paragons of moderation and placability'.

This view is so widely shared that it is interesting to note that even a more favourably disposed critic, A. Caputi, sees the end of the play as presenting Marston with a choice:

Although it is doubtful that the audience develops an intense interest in the characters of *The Malcontent*, it does develop an interest in the human relations represented. After the lying, snarling, cuckolding, and treachery of the first three acts, the chastened air that settles over the relations between characters at the end of Act IV is like the dawning of a new day. Clearly, Marston could easily have had Pietro, Ferneze, and Aurelia killed off; indeed, in an ordinary revenge play he probably would have. Instead, he has saved them for the uses just described, neglecting the seriousness

[1] P. R. Horne, *The Tragedies of Giambattista Cinthio Giraldi*, Oxford, 1962, p. 155.
[2] J. Peter, *Complaint and Satire in Early English Literature*, Oxford, 1956, p. 238.

that would proceed from their deaths in favor of the act of faith that he has achieved.[1]

This insight is the more valuable if it contributes towards an account of *The Malcontent* that properly sees its 'development' as much in terms of themes, tone and relationship as in terms of character development. *The Malcontent*, after all, is more concerned with character restoration than development, and with recovery more than revenge.

The matter of tone is both a literal and a figurative one. Hence, *The Malcontent* opens with loud discordant music, unfitting for the dignity of a court, but suitable prelude for Malevole's abusive castigation of its unworthy occupants. The play closes after the essential harmony of a skilfully executed dance by the masked avengers, a harmony enhanced by the ludicrous rehearsal of a fashionable, but unsuccessful, dance in an earlier scene. Again, Marston's preoccupation with verbal and moral dissonance in the first part of the play results in the unexpectedly satisfying use of resolved discords at the climax of the play's serious action; the two main themes of the play are united in the disguised Pietro's reconciliation with Aurelia, when the usurping duke forgives the adulterous wife. Yet the serene verbal music of the hermit's offer of sanctuary is shown to be no more than a passing achievement, until Malevole's sombre vision of man's desperate state moves Pietro beyond the limits of his personal grief into a declaration of his political guilt.

The reconciliation between Pietro and Altofronto at the end of Act IV ensures that the consummation of the play will be in accordance with this supreme achievement of moral sanity, rather than in some fresh eruption of personal and political revenge. Dramatically, of course, Malevole is the key figure; but thematically Pietro is also essential. He wronged Malevole by the act of usurpation; he has been doubly wronged by Mendoza. What remains of the moral action after the reconciliation of Pietro and Altofronto is the necessary achievement of a comparable justice by the latter. If this became sententiously obvious then theatrical tension would be lost; that it is maintained is partly due to fresh crises provoked by Mendoza's schemes to promote the mutual destruction of Pietro and Malevole and the enslavement of Maria. But though the last act of the play may seem to contribute little to the thematic development beyond the reassurance of Maria's fidelity the end of *The Malcontent* can be seen as anticlimax only if the achievement of Altofronto in keeping a similar faith with moral law is regarded as less serious an outcome

[1] *Op. cit.*, p. 198.

than would be provided by the execution of his enemies. If we
follow the theme of revenge too closely we shall overlook the moment
when it is overtaken by the counter-theme of magnanimity. If we
listen only to Malevole's threats and sententious appeals, and fail to
attend to the nature of the stratagems he employs, we shall share the
diminished responsiveness of his enemies more than the enlightened
understanding of final allies.

Coleridge once remarked that 'You may get a motto for every sect
in religion, or line of thought in morals or philosophy, from Seneca;
but nothing is ever thought *out* by him.'[1] The charge might be
extended to Marston's frequent citation of philosophical maxims
were it not that by the device of Altofronto/Malevole, Christian
prince and cynic, he has ensured not only that a wide range of
philosophical opinion is given utterance, but that we shall perceive
how much the august and disciplined ideals owe their realisation
to the effective machinations of the crude satyr figure. Some critics
have thought that Altofronto can scarcely survive the persona of
Malevole, and he does indeed weary of the role, 'O God, how loathsome this toying is to me!' (V. ii, 41): but by then the stratagem has
succeeded so well that there is no longer doubt of the final triumph,
nor is any choice left but the completion of the ritual action.

Marston has made certain that his audience will grasp the eventual
drift of the play's concern with restoration as much as with retribution by creating his moral landscape out of those ascetic images he
had used before in *Antonio's Revenge*. But now Pietro, the Hermit
of the Rocks, lamenting his own death among the basic features of a
classic natural scene—rocks, cave, sky and sea—achieves a stern
clarity, owed less to comparable landscapes of pastoral tragi-comedy
than to subterranean echoes of the *Oresteia*. When Malevole muttered
about Aegisthus, Agamemnon and their fate, he was dismissed as
gross; when he cried 'Orestes, beware Orestes' (I. v, 13) Mendoza
spurned him as a beggar. The dismissal of the warning heightens
the irony of the most elaborate deception scene in the play; for the
events of Act IV, Scene iii, in which Malevole and Pietro come in
disguise to the court of the adulterous Mendoza and Aurelia, to give
feigned report of Duke Pietro's death, borrow their strength from
that fateful visit made by the disguised Orestes and Pylades in the
Choephoroe to the court of the adulterous Aegisthus and Clytemnestra, to recount the feigned report of Orestes' death.

Malevole elsewhere uses warning prophecy, for instance when he
tries to persuade Bilioso to take his new wife with him upon his
journey as an ambassador because of the dangers she will be exposed

[1] *Table Talk*, 26 June 1830.

to if left alone in the vicious court. Malevole is clearly thinking of
the hazards to his own wife when he cries

> Ulysses absent,
> O Ithaca, can chastest Penelope hold out?   (III. ii, 49)

But though he uses a cunning akin to that of Ulysses, in rescuing
Maria from her unwelcome suitor, Malevole is no more to be
identified with Ulysses than Pietro with Orestes. The purpose of
such evocative references is to delineate the moral context and
indicate the eventual design. In particular the use in IV. iii of such a
deliberate moment from the greatest drama concerned with themes
of usurpation, adultery and tyranny, suggests the inevitability of
Marston's conclusion to his play. We know that the masquerading
Genoan dukes must ultimately submit to the same demand that the
Furies obeyed, the acclamation of a re-established justice and the
renewal of an ideal moral law known to be incompatible with the
satisfaction of violent appetites. Yet the dramatic tension of *The
Malcontent* is maintained until the end because we need to witness
the successful reconciliation of Malevole, the spitting critic, with
Altofronto, the magnanimous duke.

This final reunion is not simple, because the acquisition of the
virtue is not easily to be presumed. Caputi remarks that

> Marston's presentation of superior behaviour is always accom-
> panied by a full sense of its difficulties, of the intractability of the
> human material that must be reformed. In *The Malcontent* the
> ascendancy of Altofronto is persuasive chiefly because the play and
> Altofronto as Malevole within the play are so relentless in their
> exposure of that intractability.[1]

This reassuring intractability is in evidence right to the end, and
the last speeches remain under the double pressures of moral
idealism and political necessity. Altofronto, having spared Mendoza's
life, delivers a homily upon the true quality of a monarch, owed not
to 'birth' but to a 'glorious soul'. We are near to the presentation of
deified rule as exhibited in Italian tragedy:

> Idealization of the *magnanimo* by the Humanists reached its highest
> point in the conception of liberality and clemency as being divine
> qualities, whose possession rendered the prince God-like.[2]

But the tragedy which would justify this seriousness, and the
divine aid which might sanctify the monarch, have been excluded
from the tragi-comic world of *The Malcontent*. The humanity which
is asserted at the end would be less than recognisably human if it

[1] *Op. cit.*, p. 199.
[2] P. R. Horne, *op. cit.*, p. 157.

did not permit that expression of justifiable bitterness, when Altofronto momentarily reassumes the nature of Malevole and kicks
out Mendoza, with 'An eagle takes not flies'. To ask, as J. Peter
does, 'What sort of fly is this?', and to feel that Marston has let
Mendoza off too lightly, is to ignore the peculiar satisfaction, personal
and public, that this exemplary action affords. The fly after all is
the fly in the adage, whose contemptible capacities magnify those
of the sovereign eagle; and the satisfaction is very much of the
politically shrewd nature that was reflected upon with admiration
by Guicciardini:

> There is nothing in life more desirable or more glorious than to
> see your enemy prostrate on the ground and at your mercy. And
> this glory is doubled if you use it well, that is, by showing mercy
> and being content to have won.[1]

The malcontent accepts this manner of contentment. Altofronto's
pardoning of the petty villains immediately expiates his own petti-
ness. The corrective critic is absorbed into the effective ruler, whose
essential common humanity is revealed when even the ideal mask of
magnanimity is instantly put aside, and the player bows his way
back into the real world:

> The rest of idle actors idly part;
> And as for me, I here assume my right,

the human right, that is, to be one self again.

VI.   I. vii, 79–80

---

[1] Francesco Guicciardini, *Maxims and Reflections of a Renaissance States-
man*, trans. M. Domandi (Harper Torchbooks), 1965, p. 60. (*Ricordi* 72,
Series C.)

ILLUSTRATIONS

Plate I from Andreas Alciatus, *Emblemata* (Antwerp, 1573)
Plate II from Camillo Camilli, *Imprese illustri* (Venice, 1586)
Plates III, IV and V from Geoffrey Whitney, *A Choice of Emblems* (fac-simile reprint, ed. H. Green, London, 1866)
Plate VI from Vaenius, *Amorum Emblemata* (Antwerp, 1608)

For illustration and comment on some of Marston's knowledge of emblems see M. Praz, *Studi sul Concettismo,* who prints emblems of the eagle carrying the tortoise, from Camilli, *Imprese illustri,* and of the bear licking its cubs, from Vaenius, *Amorum emblemata,* and traces the flatterer as ungrateful ivy to emblems in Corrozet and Picinelli.

NOTE ON THE TEXT

THE COMPLEX printing history of *The Malcontent* is not easy to summarise, and some of its textual and bibliographical problems remain insoluble in view of the extant texts. But certain matters can be stated.

Three quarto editions of the play appeared in 1604, printed by Valentine Simmes. Sir W. W. Greg has collated these three editions.[1] The first edition was set from manuscript, presumably authorial and offering difficulties to the compositor; corrected and uncorrected states survive in several formes, inner B, outer E, and inner G. The second edition was set up from standing type; thus, though a prologue and epilogue were added the prologue followed the epilogue; several corrections were made, and Marston seems to have attempted some minor censorship; but the second edition also introduces problems characteristic of its printing situation, particularly in the matter of rearranged type.[2] Wine made the important discovery that the Pforzheimer Library copy of the second edition contains 'one whole sheet (G) which has been completely recast, differing from all other copies of this edition'.[3] Corrected and uncorrected states of formes B and G again remain in extant copies. The second edition is rare, presumably because the printing was abandoned when the more ambitious third edition was decided upon. In the third edition the 'Induction' was added, prologue and epilogue were relegated to the end, and many passages were added, while the whole text was reset.

The cumulative process of correction throughout this printing history enables an editor to accept some earlier readings which have been corrupted as well as some readings introduced later. A more difficult problem is presented by the omission of stage directions, and the unsure nature of some marginal interpolations.

The present text is based on a Folger Shakespeare Library copy of the third edition, collated with other copies of the third edition in the British Museum (three copies), Folger Shakespeare Library (two other copies), the British Museum copy of the second edition, the British Museum copy of the first edition, and the Folger Shakespeare Library copies of the first edition (two copies).

[1] See *A Bibliography of the English Printed Drama to the Restoration*, 1939, I, 332.
[2] See Fredson Bowers, 'Notes on Standing Type in Elizabethan Printing', *Papers of the Bibliographical Society of America* (1946), 205–24.
[3] Wine, p. xii.

The major additions to the third edition occur in the present text at the following reference points:

I. iii. 102–143	*Nay, to select . . . think it.*
I. iii. 149–165	*Farewell . . . heart.*
I. iv. 43–86	*O the . . . Castilio.*
I. viii	additional scene
V. i. 1–51	additional scene, though no scene division in quarto
V. i. 61–87	*O fool . . . Maquerelle.*
V. ii. 63–93	*Make way . . . Cornets!*
V. iii. 17–30	*Who, I? . . . puritan.*
V. iv. 132–53	*O. I have seen . . . patiently.*

In this present edition the third edition is termed Q, the first edition Q1, and the second edition Q2.

FURTHER READING

Axelrad, A. J. *Un Malcontent Elizabethain: John Marston (1576–1634)*, Paris, 1955.

Bradbrook, M. C. *Themes and Conventions of Elizabethan Tragedy*, Cambridge, 1934.

Caputi, A. *John Marston, Satirist*, Cornell, 1961.

Ellis-Fermor, U. M. *The Jacobean Drama*, revised edition, 1958.

Hunter, G. K. 'English Folly and Italian Vice', in *Jacobean Theatre (Stratford-upon-Avon Studies 1)*, 1960.

Kieffer, C. 'Music and Marston's *The Malcontent*', *Studies in Philology*, LI, 2 (1954).

Pellegrini, G. *Il Teatro di John Marston*, Pisa, 1952.

Peter, J. *Complaint and Satire in Early English Literature*, Oxford, 1956.

Praz, M. *Studi sul Concettismo*, Florence, 1946.

Salingar, L. G. 'Tourneur and the Tragedy of Revenge', in *The Age of Shakespeare* (Pelican guide), 1955.

Spencer, Theodore. 'The Elizabethan Malcontent', in *J. Q. Adams Memorial Studies*, Washington, 1948.

THE

MALCONTENT

Augmented by *Marston.*

With the Additions played by the Kings
Maiefties fervants.

Written by *Ihon Webster.*

1 6 0 4.

AT LONDON

Printed by V.S. for William Afpley, and
are to be fold at his fhop in Paules
Church-yard.

BENIAMINO IONSONIO

POETAE
ELEGANTISSIMO
GRAVISSIMO

AMICO   5
SVO CANDIDO ET CORDATO

IOHANNES MARSTON
MVSARVM ALVMNVS

ASPERAM HANC SVAM THALIAM

D.D.   10

1 BENIAMINO Q1, Q2 (BENIAMINI Q)
10 *D.D.* 'Dat Dedicatque'

1–10 'To Benjamin Jonson, most refined and serious poet, and his
sincere, wise friend, John Marston, disciple of the Muses, gives and
dedicates this his rough-comedy.'

To the Reader

I am an ill orator; and in truth, use to indite more honestly
than eloquently, for it is my custom to speak as I think, and
write as I speak.

In plainness therefore understand, that in some things I   5
have willingly erred, as in supposing a Duke of Genoa, and in
taking names different from that city's families: for which
some may wittily accuse me; but my defence shall be as honest,
as many reproofs unto me have been most malicious. Since
(I heartily protest) it was my care to write so far from reason-   10
able offence, that even strangers, in whose state I laid my
scene, should not from thence draw any disgrace to any, dead
or living. Yet in despite of my endeavours, I understand, some
have been most unadvisedly over-cunning in misinterpreting
me, and with subtlety (as deep as hell) have maliciously spread   15
ill rumours, which springing from themselves, might to themselves have heavily returned. Surely I desire to satisfy every
firm spirit, who, in all his actions, proposeth to himself no
more ends than God and virtue do, whose intentions are always
simple: to such I protest, that with my free understanding I   20
have not glanced at disgrace of any, but of those whose unquiet
studies labour innovation, contempt of holy policy, reverend,
comely superiority, and established unity: for the rest of my
supposed tartness, I fear not but unto every worthy mind it
will be approved so general and honest as may modestly pass   25
with the freedom of a satire. I would fain leave the paper; only
one thing afflicts me, to think that scenes invented merely to be
spoken should be enforcively published to be read, and that the
least hurt I can receive is to do myself the wrong. But since
others otherwise would do me more, the least inconvenience is   30
to be accepted. I have myself, therefore, set forth this comedy;
but so, that my enforced absence must much rely upon the
printer's discretion: but I shall entreat slight errors in ortho-
graphy may be as slightly overpassed; and that the unhand-
some shape which this trifle in reading presents may be   35

8 *wittily* knowingly
22 *innovation* revolution
32 *but so* in such circumstances

5

pardoned, for the pleasure it once afforded you when it was presented with the soul of lively action.

Sine aliqua dementia nullus Phoebus.

I. M.   40

39 Q, Q2 (*Me mea sequentur fata* Q1)

---

39 *Sine . . . Phoebus.* 'No poet is without some madness' (perhaps based on *Nullum magnum ingenium sine mixtura dementiae fuit,* Seneca, *De Tranq. Animi,* xvii, 10).
The replaced quotation, 'My fates follow me', may indicate Marston's interest in the Orestes theme.

Dramatis Personae

GIOVANNI ALTOFRONTO, disguised MALEVOLE, sometime Duke
of Genoa
PIETRO IACOMO, Duke of Genoa
MENDOZA, a minion to the Duchess of Pietro Iacomo 5
CELSO, a friend to Altofronto
BILIOSO, an old choleric marshal
PREPASSO, a gentleman usher
FERNEZE, a young courtier, and enamoured on the Duchess
[Aurelia] 10
FERRARDO, a minion to Duke Pietro Iacomo
EQUATO ⎫
GUERRINO ⎬ two courtiers
PASSARELLO, fool to Bilioso

AURELIA, Duchess to Duke Pietro Iacomo 15
MARIA, Duchess to Duke Altofronto
EMILIA ⎫
BIANCA ⎬ two ladies attending the Duchess [Aurelia]
MAQUERELLE, an old panderess

[CAPTAIN OF THE CITADEL 20
MERCURY, PRESENTER OF THE MASQUE
GUARDS, COURTIERS, and PAGES

Scene: Genoa

Actors of the King's Men, at the Globe Theatre, who appear in
the Induction: 25

| WILLIAM SLY | | HENRY CONDELL |
| JOHN SINKLO | RICHARD BURBAGE | JOHN LOWIN] |

14 *Passarello* Q (not in Q1, Q2)

7

The Induction

Enter W. SLY, *a* TIRE-MAN *following him with a stool*

TIRE-MAN

Sir, the gentlemen will be angry if you sit here.

SLY

Why? We may sit upon the stage at the private house. Thou dost not take me for a country gentleman, dost? Dost think I fear hissing? I'll hold my life thou took'st me for one of the players. 5

TIRE-MAN

No, sir.

SLY

By God's lid, if you had, I would have given you but six-pence for your stool. Let them that have stale suits sit in the galleries. Hiss at me! He that will be laughed out of a tavern or an ordinary shall seldom feed well or be drunk in good 10 company. Where's Harry Condell, Dick Burbage and Will Sly? Let me speak with some of them.

TIRE-MAN

An't please you to go in, sir, you may.

SLY

I tell you, no. I am one that hath seen this play often, and can give them intelligence for their action. I have most of the 15 jests here in my table-book.

Enter SINKLO

SINKLO

Save you, coz.

SLY

O cousin, come, you shall sit between my legs here.

s.d. *tire-man* dresser and property-man
  7 *lid* eye-lid (slid Q)
 10 *ordinary* eating-house
 11 *Dick* (D: Q)
    Will (W: Q)
 15 *intelligence* information
 16 *table-book* note-book

---

  2 *sit . . . house.* The habit which gallants had of sitting on the stage, whether at the private or public theatres, is best described in Dekker's *Gull's Horn-book* (1609).

9

SINKLO

No indeed, cousin, the audience then will take me for a viol-
da-gamba, and think that you play upon me.   20

SLY

Nay, rather that I work upon you, coz.

SINKLO

We stayed for you at supper last night at my cousin Honeymoon's the woollen-draper. After supper we drew cuts for a
score of apricocks, the longest cut still to draw an apricock.
By this light, 'twas Mistress Frank Honeymoon's fortune   25
still to have the longest cut: I did measure for the women.
What be these, coz?

Enter D. BURBAGE, H. CONDELL, J. LOWIN

SLY

The players. God save you.

BURBAGE

You are very welcome.

SLY

I pray you know this gentleman my cousin, 'tis Master   30
Doomsday's son, the usurer.

CONDELL

I beseech you, sir, be covered.

SLY

No, in good faith, for mine ease. Look you, my hat's the
handle to this fan. God's so, what a beast was I, I did not
leave my feather at home. Well, but I'll take an order with   35
you.

Puts his feather in his pocket

BURBAGE

Why do you conceal your feather, sir?

SLY

Why? Do you think I'll have jests broken upon me in the
play, to be laughed at? This play hath beaten all your

19–20 *viol-da-gamba* bass viol, held between the legs
23 *drew cuts* drew lots, using straws or sticks, and bawdy
34 *fan* i.e. feather
   God's so from 'Catso' (Ital. *cazzo*, penis)
35 *feather* ed. (father Q)

---

33 *for mine ease.* 'Possibly an echo of Osric's affected refusal to put on his
   hat in *Hamlet*, V. 2. 110', but also 'seems to have been a current polite
   expression' (Lucas).

gallants out of the feathers: Blackfriars hath almost spoiled   40
Blackfriars for feathers.

SINKLO

God's so, I thought 'twas for somewhat our gentlewomen at
home counselled me to wear my feather to the play, yet I am
loath to spoil it.

SLY

Why, coz?   45

SINKLO

Because I got it in the tilt-yard. There was a herald broke my
pate for taking it up, but I have worn it up and down the
Strand, and met him forty times since, and yet he dares not
challenge it.

SLY

Do you hear, sir, this play is a bitter play?   50

CONDELL

Why, sir, 'tis neither satire nor moral, but the mean passage
of a history. Yet there are a sort of discontented creatures
that bear a stingless envy to great ones, and these will wrest
the doings of any man to their base, malicious applyment.
But should their interpretation come to the test, like your   55
marmoset, they presently turn their teeth to their tail and
eat it.

SLY

I will not go so far with you, but I say, any man that hath
wit may censure (if he sit in the twelve-penny room), and I
say again, the play is bitter.   60

BURBAGE

Sir, you are like a patron that, presenting a poor scholar to a
benefice, enjoins him not to rail against anything that stands
within compass of his patron's folly. Why should not we
enjoy the ancient freedom of poesy? Shall we protest to the
ladies that their painting makes them angels, or to my   65

---

51 *mean passage* plain narration
54 *applyment* application   59 *censure* judge

40–1 *Blackfriars . . . feathers.* The acting of the play at the Blackfriars
theatre has affected the trade of the feather-makers of the locality.

56–7 *marmoset . . . it.* 'This seems a confused recollection of the beaver's
supposed habit, when hunted for its stones, of biting them off itself'
(Lucas, citing Pliny, *Naturalis Historia*, xxxii. 3).

59 *twelve-penny room.* 'A sort of large box in the lowest tier of galleries,
directly adjoining the stage' (Lucas); Dekker's *Gull's Horn-book* is
again descriptive.

young gallant that his expense in the brothel shall gain him
reputation? No sir, such vices as stand not accountable to
law should be cured as men heal tetters, by casting ink upon
them. Would you be satisfied in anything else, sir?

SLY

Ay, marry would I. I would know how you came by this play?   70

CONDELL

Faith, sir, the book was lost, and because 'twas pity so good
a play should be lost, we found it and play it.

SLY

I wonder you would play it, another company having an
interest in it?

CONDELL

Why not Malevole in folio with us, as Jeronimo in decimo-   75
sexto with them? They taught us a name for our play, we call
it *One for another*.

SLY

What are your additions?

BURBAGE

Sooth, not greatly needful, only as your sallet to your great
feast, to entertain a little more time, and to abridge the not-   80
received custom of music in our theatre. I must leave you,
sir.   *Exit* BURBAGE

SINKLO

Doth he play the Malcontent?

CONDELL

Yes, sir.

SINKLO

I durst lay four of mine ears, the play is not so well acted as   85
it hath been.

CONDELL

O no, sir, nothing *ad Parmenonis suem*.

---

68 *tetters* skin-eruptions
79 *sallet* salad
80 *entertain* pass   *abridge* cut short

70–81 See Introduction, pp. xiii–xiv.
87 *ad . . . suem*: 'compared with Parmeno's pig'. Plutarch, in *Symposiaca
    problemata*, V. i, tells of one Parmeno who used to imitate the grunting
    of a pig so well that his admirers declared the sound of a real pig as
    nothing 'compared with Parmeno's pig'. Lucas points out that Holland's
    translation of Plutarch had appeared in 1603, and that Condell here
    rebukes Sinklo for being carried away by opinion about the quality
    of the boys' acting before the men have been seen.

LOWIN

Have you lost your ears, sir, that you are so prodiga¹
laying them?

SINKLO

Why did you ask that, friend?   90

LOWIN

Marry sir, because I have heard of a fellow would offer to
lay a hundred-pound wager, that was not worth five bawbees;
and in this kind you might venture four of your elbows. Yet
God defend your coat should have so many.

SINKLO

Nay, truly, I am no great censurer, and yet I might have been   95
one of the college of critics once. My cousin here hath an
excellent memory indeed, sir.

SLY

Who, I? I'll tell you a strange thing of myself, and I can tell
you for one that never studied the art of memory, 'tis very
strange too.   100

CONDELL

What's that, sir?

SLY

Why, I'll lay a hundred pounds I'll walk but once down by
the Goldsmiths' Row in Cheap, take notice of the signs, and
tell you them with a breath instantly.

LOWIN

'Tis very strange.   105

SLY

They begin as the world did, with Adam and Eve. There's in
all just five and fifty. I do use to meditate much when I come
to plays too. What do you think might come into a man's
head now, seeing all this company?

CONDELL

I know not, sir.   110

SLY

I have an excellent thought: if some fifty of the Grecians
that were crammed in the horse belly had eaten garlic, do you
not think the Trojans might have smelt out their knavery?

94 *defend* forbid

---

92 *bawbees.* Scotch coin, equivalent to halfpenny; 'possibly an allusion to
   James's needy Scotch followers' (Lucas).
107 *five and fifty*: 'ten fair dwelling-houses and fourteen shops' according
   to Stow's reckoning (Dyce).
111 *an excellent thought*: prompted by garlic fumes.

CONDELL
   Very likely.
SLY
   By God, I would they had, for I love Hector horribly.   115
SINKLO
   O but coz, coz—
   'Great Alexander, when he came to the tomb of Achilles,
   Spake with a big loud voice, "O thou thrice blessed and
   happy".'
SLY
   Alexander was an ass to speak so well of a filthy cullion.   120
LOWIN
   Good sir, will you leave the stage? I'll help you to a private
   room.
SLY
   Come, coz, let's take some tobacco. Have you never a pro-
   logue?
LOWIN
   Not any, sir.   125
SLY
   Let me see, I will make one extempore. Come to them, and
   fencing of a congee with arms and legs, be round with them
   —'Gentlemen, I could wish for the women's sakes you had
   all soft cushions: and gentlewomen, I could wish that for the
   men's sakes you had all more easy standings'. What would   130
   they wish more but the play now? And that they shall have
   instantly.   *Exeunt*

         An imperfect ode, being but one staff,
              spoken by the Prologue
      To wrest each hurtless thought to private sense
         Is the foul use of ill-bred impudence:
            Immodest censure now grows wild,   5
               All over-running.
            Let innocence be ne'er so chaste,

---

115 *they* ed. (he Q)   127 *fencing of a congee* performing an elaborate bow
title *staff* stanza

117–19 *Great . . . happy.* Sinklo's version of John Harvey's hexameters:

   Noble *Alexander*, when he came to the tomb of *Achilles*,
   Sighing spake with a bigge voice: O thrice blessed *Achilles*':

this version of Petrarch, Sonnet CLIII, was printed in Gabriel Harvey's
Three proper, and wittie, familiar Letters to Spenser (1580).

Yet at the last
She is defiled,
With too nice-brained cunning.   10
O you of fairer soul,
Control,
With an Herculean arm,
This harm;
And once teach all old freedom of a pen,   15
Which still must write of fools, while'st writes of men.

THE MALCONTENT

Vexat censura columbas

Act I, Scene i

The vilest out-of-tune music being heard
Enter BILIOSO *and* PREPASSO

BILIOSO
Why, how now? Are ye mad, or drunk, or both, or what?
PREPASSO
Are ye building Babylon there?
BILIOSO
Here's a noise in court, you think you are in a tavern, do you
not?
PREPASSO
You think you are in a brothel-house, do you not? This   5
room is ill-scented.

Enter one with a perfume

So, perfume, perfume; some upon me, I pray thee. The duke
is upon instant entrance; so, make place there.

title *censura* Q1, Q (*censurae* Q2)

---

title *Vexat . . . columbas.* Juvenal, *Satires*, II, 63. 'The context is Laronia's
defence of women by citing male offences: "de nobis post haec tristis
sententia fertur? dat veniam corvis, vexat censura columbas." "After
these things what evil judgment can be put on us women. [The criti-
cising male] absolves the crows and passes judgment on the doves".'
(Harrier.) This motto introduces Malevole's attack on the courtiers.

Act I, Scene ii

Enter the DUKE PIETRO, FERRARDO, COUNT EQUATO,
COUNT CELSO *before, and* GUERRINO

PIETRO
Where breathes that music?

BILIOSO
The discord rather than the music is heard from the malcontent Malevole's chamber.

FERRARDO
Malevole!

MALEVOLE
(*Out of his chamber*) Yaugh, God o' man, what dost thou   5
there? Duke's Ganymede, Juno's jealous of thy long stockings. Shadow of a woman, what wouldst, weasel? Thou lamb
o' court, what dost thou bleat for? Ah, you smooth-chinned
catamite!

PIETRO
Come down, thou ragged cur, and snarl here. I give thy   10
dogged sullenness free liberty; trot about and bespurtle
whom thou pleasest.

MALEVOLE
I'll come among you, you goatish-blooded toderers, as
gum into taffeta, to fret, to fret. I'll fall like a sponge into
water, to suck up, to suck up. Howl again. I'll go to church,   15
and come to you.   [*Exit*]

PIETRO
This Malevole is one of the most prodigious affections that

  5 (*Out of his chamber*) probably upper-stage
  6 *Ganymede* a son of Troas, ravished away for his beauty to be
    cup-bearer to Zeus
  7 *lamb* favourite
  9 *catamite* male prostitute
 10 *ragged* Q (rugged Q1, Q2)
 11 *bespurtle* bespatter
 14 *gum . . . fret* inferior or defective taffeta was gummed; hence
    it frayed or 'fretted'
 15 *church* Q, Q2 (I'll pray Q1)
 17 *affections* dispositions

  7 *Shadow of a woman.* Inverted commonplace: see Ben Jonson's song
    'That women are but men's shadows'.
 13 *toderers.* The word clearly indicates libertinism, though its etymology
    is obscure; a 'tod' is a fox.

ever conversed with nature; a man, or rather a monster, more
discontent than Lucifer when he was thrust out of the
presence. His appetite is insatiable as the grave, as far from   20
any content as from heaven. His highest delight is to procure
others' vexation, and therein he thinks he truly serves
heaven; for 'tis his position, whosoever in this earth can be
contented is a slave and damned; therefore does he afflict all
in that to which they are most affected. The elements   25
struggle within him; his own soul is at variance within herself. His speech is halter-worthy at all hours. I like him,
faith, he gives good intelligence to my spirit, makes me
understand those weaknesses which others' flattery palliates.
Hark, they sing.   30

Act I, Scene iii

[A song]
Enter MALEVOLE *after the song*

[PIETRO]
See, he comes. Now shall you hear the extremity of a malcontent. He is as free as air; he blows over every man.—And
sir, whence come you now?

MALEVOLE
From the public place of much dissimulation, the church.

PIETRO
What didst there?   5

MALEVOLE
Talk with a usurer; take up at interest.

PIETRO
I wonder what religion thou art of?

MALEVOLE
Of a soldier's religion.

PIETRO
And what dost think makes most infidels now?

MALEVOLE
Sects, sects. I have seen seeming Piety change her robe so   10
oft that sure none but some arch-devil can shape her a new
petticoat.

23 *position* argument
26–7 *within herself* Q (not in Q1, Q2)
4 *the church* Q (not in Q2; deleted from majority of extant copies
    of Q1; see Wine, p. 18)
6 *take up* borrow
11 *new* Q1, Q2 (not in Q)

PIETRO

O, a religious policy.

MALEVOLE

But damnation on a politic religion! I am weary—would I
were one of the duke's hounds now.   15

PIETRO

But what's the common news abroad, Malevole? Thou
dogg'st rumour still.

MALEVOLE

Common news? Why, common words are, 'God save ye',
'Fare ye well'; common actions, flattery and cosenage; common things, women and cuckolds. And how does my little   20
Ferrard? Ah, ye lecherous animal, my little ferret, he goes
sucking up and down the palace into every hen's nest like
a weasel. And to what dost thou addict thy time to now,
more than to those antique painted drabs that are still
affected of young courtiers, Flattery, Pride, and Venery?   25

FERRARDO

I study languages. Who dost think to be the best linguist of
our age?

MALEVOLE

Phew! the devil. Let him possess thee, he'll teach thee to
speak all languages most readily and strangely; and great
reason, marry, he's travelled greatly i' the world, and is   30
everywhere.

FERRARDO

Save i' the court.

MALEVOLE

Ay, save i' the court. (*To* BILIOSO) And how does my old
muckhill overspread with fresh snow? Thou half a man, half
a goat, all a beast! How does thy young wife, old huddle?   35

BILIOSO

Out, you improvident rascal!

14–15 *I . . . now* Q, Q2 (not in Q1)
19 *cosenage* cheating
35 *huddle* miserly old man

28–31 *Phew! . . . everywhere.* Diabolic possession was supposed to bring
  the gift of tongues; see Jonson's *The Devil is an Ass*, V. v. (Wood).
33–4 *And . . . snow?* Cf. 'Yon's but a muckhill ouer-spred with snow',
  The Scourge of Villanie VII, 'A Cynick Satyr' 154; there are other
  self-borrowings from this satire.
34–5 *Thou . . . beast!* Cf. 'Oh villaine indiscreet, vnseasonable. Halfe a man
  halfe a goat, and all a beast' (*Il pastor fido*, II. vi, 1602, trans. Sig. G).

MALEVOLE

Do, kick, thou hugely-horned old duke's ox, good Master
Make-Pleas.

PIETRO

How dost thou live nowadays, Malevole?

MALEVOLE

Why, like the knight, Sir Patrick Penlolians, with killing o'   40
spiders for my lady's monkey.

PIETRO

How dost spend the night, I hear thou never sleep'st?

MALEVOLE

O no, but dream the most fantastical. O Heaven! O fubbery,
fubbery!

PIETRO

Dream? What dream'st?   45

MALEVOLE

Why, methinks I see that signior pawn his foot-cloth, that
metreza her plate; this madam takes physic that t'other
monsieur may minister to her; here is a pander jewelled;
there is a fellow in shift of satin this day that could not
shift a shirt t'other night; here a Paris supports that Helen,   50
there's a Lady Guinever bears up that Sir Lancelot. Dreams,
dreams, visions, fantasies, chimeras, imaginations, tricks,
conceits! (*To* PREPASSO) Sir Tristram Trimtram, come aloft,
Jackanapes, with a whim-wham; here's a knight of the land

---

38 *Make-Pleas* (Make-pleece Qq; Make-Please Wine)
43 *fubbery* deceit   46 *foot-cloth* caparizon
47 *metreza* mistress (Ital.)   49 *shift* change
53–4 *come aloft, Jackanapes* ape-ward's cry
54 *whim-wham* trifle ('reduplication with vowel-variation, like
flim-flam, trim-tram' O.E.D.)

---

40 *Sir Patrick Penlolians.* Q, Q2 (Penlohans Q1 corrected; Penlobrans Q1
uncorrected; Wine). Probably Marston was continuing his typified
nomenclature; Florio offers 'Pendule labbra, bigge, downe-hanging
blabbered-lips'; there is 'the Irish Lord, S. Patrick' in *The Dutch
Courtesan,* II. i.

40–1 *killing ... monkey.* Bawdy; cf. Petulant's sneer to Witwoud 'Carry
your Mistress's Monkey a Spider', *The Way of the World,* IV. ix.

54–8 *knight ... huge.* 'Catito' is a coinage from 'cat', or 'tipcat', a boys'
game, which like 'trap' or 'trapball', and riding at the ring (a form of
jousting in which the rider tried to put his lance through a suspended
ring), offer themselves readily to Malevole's suggestiveness about the
courtiers' immorality. 'Lancelot' and 'Lady Guinevere' had already
become type-names for debauched chivalry.

of Catito shall play at trap with any page in Europe; do the   55
sword-dance with any morris-dancer in Christendom; ride
at the ring till the fin of his eyes look as blue as the welkin,
and run the wild-goose chase even with Pompey the huge.

PIETRO
You run—

MALEVOLE
To the devil. Now, Signior Guerrino, that thou from a most   60
pitied prisoner shouldst grow a most loathed flatterer! Alas,
poor Celso, thy star's oppressed; thou art an honest lord,
'tis pity.

EQUATO
Is't pity?

MALEVOLE
Ay, marry is't, philosophical Equato, and 'tis pity that thou,   65
being so excellent a scholar by art, shouldst be so ridiculous
a fool by nature. I have a thing to tell you, Duke; bid 'em
avaunt, bid 'em avaunt.

PIETRO
Leave us, leave us.
                    Exeunt all saving PIETRO *and* MALEVOLE
Now, sir, what is't?   70

MALEVOLE
Duke, thou art a becco, a cornuto.

PIETRO
How!

MALEVOLE
Thou art a cuckold.

PIETRO
Speak! Unshale him quick.

MALEVOLE
With most tumbler-like nimbleness.   75

PIETRO
Who? By whom? I burst with desire.

MALEVOLE
Mendoza is the man makes thee a horned beast. Duke, 'tis
Mendoza cornutes thee.

PIETRO
What conformance? Relate! short, short!

57 *fin* rim
62 *oppressed* in decline
71 *becco, cornuto* cuckold (Ital.)
74 *Unshale* unshell, disclose
79 *conformance* confirmation

MALEVOLE

As a lawyer's beard.   80
'There is an old crone in the court, her name is Maquerelle,
      She is my mistress, sooth to say, and she doth ever tell me.'
Blurt o' rhyme, blurt o' rhyme! Maquerelle is a cunning
bawd, I am an honest villain, thy wife is a close drab, and
thou art a notorious cuckold. Farewell, Duke.   85

PIETRO

Stay, stay.

MALEVOLE

Dull, dull Duke, can lazy patience make lame revenge?
O God, for a woman to make a man that which God never
created, never made!

PIETRO

What did God never make?   90

MALEVOLE

A cuckold. To be made a thing that's hoodwinked with
kindness, whilst every rascal fillips his brows; to have a coxcomb with egregious horns pinned to a lord's back, every
page sporting himself with delightful laughter, whilst he
must be the last must know it—pistols and poniards, pistols   95
and poniards!

PIETRO

Death and damnation!

MALEVOLE

Lightning and thunder!

PIETRO

Vengeance and torture!

MALEVOLE

Catzo!   100

PIETRO

O, revenge!

MALEVOLE

Nay, to select among ten thousand fairs
A lady far inferior to the most,
In fair proportion both of limb and soul;
To take her from austerer check of parents,   105
To make her his by most devoutful rites,
Make her commandress of a better essence
Than is the gorgeous world even of a man;

83 *Blurt* expletive ('a fig for' *O.E.D.*)
84 *close drab* secret whore
92–3 *coxcomb* fool's-cap
100 *Catzo!* penis (Ital. *cazzo*)

To hug her with as raised an appetite
As usurers do their delved-up treasury,   110
(Thinking none tells it but his private self);
To meet her spirit in a nimble kiss,
Distilling panting ardour to her heart;
True to her sheets, nay, diets strong his blood,
To give her height of hymeneal sweets—   115

PIETRO

O God!

MALEVOLE

Whilst she lisps, and gives him some court *quelquechose*,
Made only to provoke, not satiate;
And yet, even then the thaw of her delight
Flows from lewd heat of apprehension,   120
Only from strange imagination's rankness,
That forms the adulterer's presence in her soul,
And makes her think she clips the foul knave's loins.

PIETRO

Affliction to my blood's root!

MALEVOLE

Nay think, but think what may proceed of this; adultery is   125
often the mother of incest.

PIETRO

Incest?

MALEVOLE

Yes, incest. Mark—Mendoza of his wife begets perchance a
daughter. Mendoza dies. His son marries this daughter. Say
you? Nay, 'tis frequent, not only probable, but no question 130
often acted, whilst ignorance, fearless ignorance, clasps his
own seed.

PIETRO

Hideous imagination!

MALEVOLE

Adultery? Why, next to the sin of simony 'tis the most
horrid transgression under the cope of salvation!   135

PIETRO

Next to simony?

MALEVOLE

Ay, next to simony, in which our men in next age shall not
sin.

111 *tells* counts
117 *quelquechose* dainty, unsubstantial morsel
123 *clips* embraces
135 *cope of salvation* heaven

PIETRO
  Not sin? Why?
MALEVOLE
  Because (thanks to some churchmen) our age will leave them   140
  nothing to sin with. But adultery—O dullness!—should
  show exemplary punishment, that intemperate bloods may
  freeze but to think it. I would dam him and all his genera-
  tion, my own hands should do it. Ha! I would not trust
  heaven with my vengeance anything.   145
PIETRO
  Anything, anything, Malevole! Thou shalt see instantly
  what temper my spirit holds. Farewell; remember I forget
  thee not; farewell.   *Exit* PIETRO
MALEVOLE
  Farewell.
  Lean thoughtfulness, a sallow meditation,
  Suck thy veins dry! Distemperance rob thy sleep!   150
  The heart's disquiet is revenge most deep.
  He that gets blood, the life of flesh but spills,
  But he that breaks heart's peace, the dear soul kills.
  Well, this disguise doth yet afford me that
  Which kings do seldom hear, or great men use—   155
  Free speech. And though my state's usurped,
  Yet this affected strain gives me a tongue
  As fetterless as is an emperor's.
  I may speak foolishly, ay, knavishly,
  Always carelessly, yet no one thinks it fashion   160
  To poise my breath; for he that laughs and strikes
  Is lightly felt, or seldom struck again.
  Duke, I'll torment thee; now my just revenge
  From thee than crown a richer gem shall part.
  Beneath God, naught's so dear as a calm heart.   165

Act I, Scene iv

Enter CELSO

CELSO
  My honoured lord—
MALEVOLE
  Peace, speak low! Peace, O Celso, constant lord,

141–2 *should show* ed. (shue should Q)
143 *dam* choke
150 *Distemperance* mental or physical disturbance
161 *poise* weigh

Thou to whose faith I only rest discovered,
Thou, one of full ten millions of men,
That lovest virtue only for itself,   5
Thou, in whose hands old Ops may put her soul,
Behold forever-banished Altofront,
This Genoa's last year's duke. O truly noble,
I wanted those old instruments of state,
Dissemblance and suspect. I could not time it, Celso;   10
My throne stood like a point in midst of a circle,
To all of equal nearness; bore with none;
Reigned all alike; so slept in fearless virtue,
Suspectless, too suspectless; till the crowd,
Still lickerous of untried novelties,   15
Impatient with severer government,
Made strong with Florence, banished Altofront.

CELSO

Strong with Florence! Ay, thence your mischief rose;
For when the daughter of the Florentine
Was matched once with this Pietro, now duke,   20
No stratagem of state untried was left,
Till you of all—

MALEVOLE   Of all was quite bereft.

Alas, Maria too, close prisoned,
My true-faith'd duchess, i' the citadel.

CELSO

I'll still adhere; let's mutiny and die.   25

MALEVOLE

O no! Climb not a falling tower, Celso,
'Tis well held desperation, no zeal,
Hopeless to strive with fate. Peace! Temporise.
Hope, hope, that never forsak'st the wretched'st man,
Yet bidd'st me live, and lurk in this disguise.   30
What, play I well the free-breathed discontent?
Why, man, we are all philosophical monarchs or natural
fools. Celso, the court's afire; the duchess' sheets will smoke
for't ere it be long. Impure Mendoza, that sharp-nosed lord,
that made the cursed match linked Genoa with Florence,   35
now broad-horns the duke, which he now knows. Discord to
malcontents is very manna; when the ranks are burst, then
scuffle Altofront.

6 *Ops* goddess of plenty
9 *wanted* lacked   10 *time it* temporise
12 *bore with* favoured   15 *lickerous of* eager for
17 *Made strong* allied   20 *this* ed. (his Q)

CELSO
Ay, but durst?

MALEVOLE
'Tis gone; 'tis swallowed like a mineral;   40
Some way t'will work—Phewt! I'll not shrink.
He's resolute who can no lower sink.

BILIOSO *entering,* MALEVOLE *shifteth his speech*

O the father of maypoles! Did you never see a fellow whose
whole strength consisted in his breath, respect in his office,
religion in his lord, and love in himself? Why then, behold.   45

BILIOSO
Signior.

MALEVOLE
My right worshipful lord: your court night-cap makes you
have a passing high forehead.

BILIOSO
I can tell you strange news, but I am sure you know them
already; the duke speaks much good of you.   50

MALEVOLE
Go to, then; and shall you and I now enter into a strict
friendship?

BILIOSO
Second one another?

MALEVOLE
Yes.

BILIOSO
Do one another good offices?   55

MALEVOLE
Just. What though I called thee old ox, egregious wittol,
broken-bellied coward, rotten mummy? Yet, since I am in
favour—

BILIOSO
Words of course, terms of disport. His grace presents you
by me a chain, as his grateful remembrance for—I am   60
ignorant for what. Marry, ye may impart. Yet howsoever—
come—dear friend. Dost know my son?

MALEVOLE
Your son?

BILIOSO
He shall eat woodcocks, dance jigs, make possets, and play

40 *mineral* medicine   45 *religion in* ed. (religion on Q)
56 *wittol* cuckold
64 *possets* hot drinks of milk curdled with liquor and spiced

at shuttlecock with any young lord about the court. He   65
has as sweet a lady, too; dost know her little bitch?

MALEVOLE

'Tis a dog, man.

BILIOSO

Believe me, a she-bitch! O 'tis a good creature; thou shalt
be her servant. I'll make thee acquainted with my young
wife too. What, I keep her not at court for nothing. 'Tis   70
grown to supper time; come to my table; that, anything I
have, stands open to thee.

MALEVOLE

(*To* CELSO) How smooth to him that is in state of grace,
How servile is the rugged'st courtier's face.
What profit, nay what nature would keep down,   75
Are heaved to them are minions to a crown.
Envious ambition never sates his thirst,
Till, sucking all, he swells and swells, and bursts.

BILIOSO

I shall now leave you with my always-best wishes, only let's
hold betwixt us a firm correspondence, a mutual-friendly-   80
reciprocal-kind of steady-unanimous-heartily-leagued—

MALEVOLE

Did your signiorship ne'er see a pigeon-house that was
smooth, round and white without, and full of holes and stink
within? Ha' ye not, old courtier?

BILIOSO

O yes, 'tis the form, the fashion of them all.   85

MALEVOLE

Adieu, my true court-friend; farewell, my dear Castilio.

Exit BILIOSO

CELSO

Yonder's Mendoza.

MALEVOLE

(*Descries* MENDOZA) True, the privy key.

CELSO

I take my leave, sweet lord.   *Exit* CELSO

MALEVOLE   'Tis fit, away!

69 *servant* lover
76 *are* who are
80 *correspondence* agreement
86 *Castilio* Baldassare Castiglione
87 *privy key* bawdy allusion to intimacy

Act I, Scene v

Enter MENDOZA, *with three or four suitors*

MENDOZA

Leave your suits with me; I can and will. Attend my secretary; leave me.   [*Exeunt suitors*]

MALEVOLE

Mendoza, hark ye, hark ye. You are a treacherous villain.
God b' wi' ye.

MENDOZA

Out, you base-born rascal!   5

MALEVOLE

We are all the sons of heaven, though a tripe-wife were our
mother. Ah, you whoreson, hot-reined he-marmoset! Aegisthus!—didst ever hear of one Aegisthus?

MENDOZA

'Gisthus?

MALEVOLE

Ay, Aegisthus; he was a filthy incontinent fleshmonger, such   10
a one as thou art.

MENDOZA

Out, grumbling rogue!

MALEVOLE

Orestes, beware Orestes!

MENDOZA

Out, beggar!

MALEVOLE

I once shall rise.   15

MENDOZA

Thou rise?

MALEVOLE

Ay, at the resurrection.
No vulgar seed but once may rise, and shall;
No king so huge, but 'fore he die may fall.   *Exit*

MENDOZA

Now, good Elysium, what a delicious heaven is it for a man   20
to be in a prince's favour! O sweet God! O pleasure! O
fortune! O all thou best of life! What should I think, what
say, what do? To be a favourite, a minion! To have a general

---

6 *tripe-wife* tripe-seller
7 *hot-reined* lascivious
7–8 *Aegisthus* Clytemnestra's lover, who cuckolded Agamemnon
13 *Orestes* Agamemnon's son, and his avenger

timorous respect observe a man, a stateful silence in his
presence, solitariness in his absence, a confused hum and   25
busy murmur of obsequious suitors training him; the cloth
held up, and way proclaimed before him; petitionary vassals
licking the pavement with their slavish knees, whilst some odd
palace-lamprels that engender with snakes, and are full of
eyes on both sides, with a kind of insinuated humbleness fix   30
all their delights upon his brow. O blessed state, what a
ravishing prospect doth the Olympus of favour yield! Death,
I cornute the duke! Sweet women, most sweet ladies—nay,
angels! By heaven, he is more accursed than a devil that
hates you, or is hated by you; and happier than a god that   35
loves you, or is beloved by you. You preservers of mankind,
life-blood of society, who would live—nay, who can live
without you? O paradise, how majestical is your austerer
presence! How imperiously chaste is your more modest face!
But, O, how full of ravishing attraction is your pretty,   40
petulant, languishing, lasciviously-composed countenance!
These amorous smiles, those soul-warming sparkling
glances, ardent as those flames that singed the world by
heedless Phaeton. In body how delicate, in soul how witty,
in discourse how pregnant, in life how wary, in favours how   45
judicious, in day how sociable, and in night how—O
pleasure unutterable! Indeed, it is most certain, one man
cannot deserve only to enjoy a beauteous woman. But a
duchess? In despite of Phoebus I'll write a sonnet instantly
in praise of her.   *Exit*   50

Act I, Scene vi

Enter FERNEZE *ushering* AURELIA, EMILIA *and* MAQUERELLE
bearing up her train, BIANCA *attending: all go out but* AURELIA,
MAQUERELLE, *and* FERNEZE

AURELIA
    And is't possible? Mendoza slight me, possible?

24 *observe* defer to
    stateful dignified
26 *training* following in his train
29 *lamprels* young lampreys
33 *cornute* make cuckold
44 *Phaeton* Phaeton lost control of the horses of the sun and was
    slain by Zeus with a thunderbolt
49 *Phoebus* Phoebus Apollo, god of poetry

FERNEZE

Possible? What can be strange in him that's drunk with
favour, grows insolent with grace? Speak, Maquerelle, speak.

MAQUERELLE

To speak feelingly, more, more richly in solid sense than
worthless words, give me those jewels of your ears to receive   5
my enforced duty. As for my part, (FERNEZE *privately feeds*
MAQUERELLE'S *hands with jewels during this speech*) 'tis well
known I can put up anything, can bear patiently with any
man; but when I heard he wronged your precious sweetness,
I was enforced to take deep offence. 'Tis most certain he   10
loves Emilia with high appetite; and, as she told me (as you
know, we women impart our secrets one to another) when she
repulsed his suit, in that he was possessed with your
endeared grace, Mendoza most ingratefully renounced all
faith to you.   15

FERNEZE

Nay, called you—speak, Maquerelle, speak.

MAQUERELLE

By heaven, 'witch!' 'dried biscuit!', and contested blush-
lessly he loved you but for a spurt or so.

FERNEZE

For maintenance.

MAQUERELLE

Advancement and regard.   20

AURELIA

O villain! O impudent Mendoza!

MAQUERELLE

Nay, he is the rustiest-jawed, the foulest-mouthed knave in
railing against our sex. He will rail against women—

AURELIA

How? How?

MAQUERELLE

I am ashamed to speak't, I.   25

AURELIA

I love to hate him, speak.

MAQUERELLE

Why, when Emilia scorned his base unsteadiness, the black-
throated rascal scolded, and said—

AURELIA

What?

8 *put up* Q1 (put Q, Q2); bawdy
22 *jawed* ed. (iade Q, iawde Q1, Q2)

MAQUERELLE
> Troth, 'tis too shameless.   30

AURELIA
> What said he?

MAQUERELLE
> Why, that at four women were fools, at fourteen drabs, at
> forty bawds, at fourscore witches, and at a hundred, cats.

AURELIA
> O unlimitable impudency!

FERNEZE
> But as for poor Ferneze's fixed heart,   35
> Was never shadeless meadow drier parched
> Under the scorching heat of heaven's dog
> Than is my heart with your enforcing eyes.

MAQUERELLE
> A hot simile.

FERNEZE
> Your smiles have been my heaven, your frowns my hell,   40
> O pity, then; grace should with beauty dwell.

MAQUERELLE
> Reasonable perfect, by'r lady.

AURELIA
> I will love thee, be it but in despite
> Of that Mendoza. 'Witch!' Ferneze, 'witch!'—
> Ferneze, thou art the duchess' favourite;   45
> Be faithful, private; but 'tis dangerous.

FERNEZE
> His love is lifeless, that for love fears breath;
> The worst that's due to sin, O would 'twere death.

AURELIA
> Enjoy my favour. I will be sick instantly and take physic;
> therefore, in depth of night visit—   50

MAQUERELLE
> Visit her chamber, but conditionally, you shall not offend
> her bed. By this diamond.

---

33 *and at a* ed. (and a Qq)
37 *heaven's dog* Sirius
38 *enforcing* compelling
51 *conditionally* on condition

47–8 *His . . . death.* Cf. *Il pastor fido*, III. iv:

> she loues too little that feares death
> Would gods death were the worst that's due to sin (Sig H3v).

FERNEZE
  By this diamond.   *Gives it to* MAQUERELLE
MAQUERELLE
  Nor tarry longer than you please. By this ruby.
FERNEZE
  By this ruby.   *Gives again*   55
MAQUERELLE
  And that the door shall not creak.
FERNEZE
  And that the door shall not creak.
MAQUERELLE
  Nay, but swear.
FERNEZE
  By this purse.   *Gives her his purse*
MAQUERELLE
  Go to; I'll keep your oaths for you: remember, visit.   60

Enter MENDOZA, *reading a sonnet*

AURELIA
  'Dried biscuit!' Look where the base wretch comes.
MENDOZA
  'Beauty's life, heaven's model, love's queen'—
MAQUERELLE
  That's his Emilia.
MENDOZA
  'Nature's triumph, best on earth'—
MAQUERELLE
  Meaning Emilia.   65
MENDOZA
  'Thou only wonder that the world hath seen'—
MAQUERELLE
  That's Emilia.
AURELIA
  Must I then hear her praised? Mendoza!
MENDOZA
  Madam, your excellency is graciously encountered; I have
  been writing passionate flashes in honour of— *Exit* FERNEZE   70
AURELIA
  Out, villain, villain!
  O judgement, where have been my eyes? What
  Bewitched election made me dote on thee?

70 *flashes* outbursts
73 *election* choice

What sorcery made me love thee? But begone,
Bury thy head. O that I could do more   75
Than loathe thee! Hence, worst of ill!
No reason ask, our reason is our will.

Exit with MAQUERELLE

MENDOZA

Women? Nay, Furies! Nay, worse, for they torment only the
bad, but women good and bad. Damnation of mankind!
Breath, hast thou praised them for this? And is't you,   80
Ferneze, are wriggled into smock-grace? Sit sure. O that I
could rail against these monsters in nature, models of hell,
curse of the earth, women that dare attempt anything, and
what they attempt they care not how they accomplish;
without all premeditation or prevention, rash in asking,   85
desperate in working, impatient in suffering, extreme in
desiring, slaves unto appetite, mistresses in dissembling,
only constant in unconstancy, only perfect in counter-
feiting; their words are feigned, their eyes forged, their
sighs dissembled, their looks counterfeit, their hair false,   90
their given hopes deceitful, their very breath artificial. Their
blood is their only god. Bad clothes and old age are only the
devils they tremble at. That I could rail now!

Act I, Scene vii

Enter PIETRO, *his sword drawn*

PIETRO

A mischief fill thy throat, thou foul-jawed slave!
Say thy prayers.

MENDOZA   I ha' forgot 'em.

PIETRO   Thou shalt die.

MENDOZA

So shalt thou. I am heart-mad.

PIETRO   I am horn-mad.

MENDOZA

Extreme mad?

---

77 *ask* Q (else Q1, Q2)
81 *smock-grace* intimate favour
85 *prevention* anticipation
89 *forged* cosmetically enhanced
90 *sighs* ed. (sights Q)
 3 *heart-mad* distracted
   horn-mad enraged; also cuckolded

PIETRO   Monstrously mad.
MENDOZA   Why?
PIETRO
  Why? Thou, thou hast dishonoured my bed.   5
MENDOZA
  I? Come, come, sit. Here's my bare heart to thee,
  As steady as is this centre to the glorious world;
  And yet, hark, thou art a cornuto—but by me?
PIETRO
  Yes, slave, by thee.
MENDOZA
  Do not, do not, with tart and spleenful breath,   10
  Lose him can lose thee. I offend my duke?
  Bear record, O ye dumb and raw-aired nights,
  How vigilant my sleepless eyes have been
  To watch the traitor; record, thou spirit of truth,
  With what debasement I ha' thrown myself   15
  To under-offices, only to learn
  The truth, the party, time, the means, the place,
  By whom, and when, and where, thou wert disgraced!
  And am I paid with 'slave!'? Hath my intrusion
  To places private and prohibited,   20
  Only to observe the closer passages—
  Heaven knows with vows of revelation—
  Made me suspected, made me deemed a villain?
  What rogue hath wronged us?
PIETRO   Mendoza, I may err.
MENDOZA
  Err? 'Tis too mild a name. But err and err,   25
  Run giddy with suspect, 'fore through me thou know
  That which most creatures save thyself do know—
  Nay, since my service hath so loathed reject,
  'Fore I'll reveal, shalt find them clipped together.
PIETRO
  Mendoza, thou know'st I am a most plain-breasted man.   30
MENDOZA
  The fitter to make cuckold. Would your brows were most
  plain too!
PIETRO
  Tell me; indeed I heard thee rail—

---

7 *centre* earth   16 *under-offices* menial occupations
21 *closer passages* secret incidents   26 *suspect* suspicion
28 *reject* rejection

MENDOZA

    At women, true. Why, what cold phlegm could choose,
    Knowing a lord so honest, virtuous,   35
    So boundless-loving, bounteous, fair-shaped, sweet,
    To be condemned, abused, defamed, made cuckold?
    Heart! I hate all women for't: sweet sheets, wax lights,
    antique bed-posts, cambric smocks, villainous curtains,
    arras pictures, oiled hinges, and all the tongue-tied lascivi-   40
    ous witnesses of great creatures' wantonness. What salvation
    can you expect?

PIETRO

    Wilt thou tell me?

MENDOZA

    Why, you may find it yourself; observe, observe.

PIETRO

    I ha' not the patience. Wilt thou deserve me? Tell, give it.   45

MENDOZA

    Tak't. Why, Ferneze is the man, Ferneze. I'll prove't; this
    night you shall take him in your sheets. Will't serve?

PIETRO

    It will; my bosom's in some peace. Till night—

MENDOZA

    What?

PIETRO

    Farewell.   50

MENDOZA

    God! How weak a lord are you!
    Why, do you think there is no more but so?

PIETRO

    Why?

MENDOZA

    Nay, then will I presume to counsel you.
    It should be thus: you, with some guard, upon the sudden   55
    Break into the princess' chamber; I stay behind,
    Without the door through which he needs must pass;
    Ferneze flies—let him; to me he comes; he's killed
    By me—observe, by me. You follow; I rail,
    And seem to save the body. Duchess comes,   60
    On whom (respecting her advancèd birth
    And your fair nature) I know—nay, I do know—
    No violence must be used. She comes; I storm,
    I praise, excuse Ferneze, and still maintain

34 *phlegm* dullness   40 *arras* tapestry
45 *deserve* earn desert or reward from

The duchess' honour; she for this loves me;   65
I honour you, shall know her soul, you mine;
Then naught shall she contrive in vengeance
(As women are most thoughtful in revenge)
Of her Ferneze, but you shall sooner know't
Than she can think't. Thus shall his death come sure;   70
Your duchess brain-caught; so, your life secure.

PIETRO
It is too well, my bosom and my heart:
When nothing helps, cut off the rotten part.   *Exit*

MENDOZA
Who cannot feign friendship can ne'er produce the effects of
hatred. Honest fool duke, subtle lascivious duchess, silly   75
novice Ferneze—I do laugh at ye! My brain is in labour till
it produce mischief, and I feel sudden throes, proofs sensible
the issue is at hand.
As bears shape young, so I'll form my devise,
Which grown, proves horrid; vengeance makes men wise.   80
                                                     [Exit]

[Act I, Scene viii]

Enter MALEVOLE *and* PASSARELLO

MALEVOLE
Fool, most happily encountered; can'st sing, fool?

PASSARELLO
Yes, I can sing, fool, if you'll bear the burden; and I can play
upon instruments, scurvily, as gentlemen do. O that I had

71 *brain-caught* tricked   75 *silly* naive (seely Q)
77 *sensible* evident   2 *bear the burden* sing the refrain

74–5 *Who . . . hatred.* Cf. *Il pastor fido*, II. iv:

Who cannot friendship faine,
Cannot truly hate. (Sig. Fv).

79–80 *As . . . horrid.* Cf. *Il pastor fido*, III. vi:

For as the Beare is wont with licking to giue shape
To her mishapen brood, that else were helplesse borne,
Eu'n so a Louer to his bare desire,
That in the birth was shapeless, weake and fraile,
Giuing but forme and strength begetteth loue:
Which whilst t'is young and tender, then t'is sweet,
But waxing to more yeares, more cruell growes,
That in the end (Mirtillo) an inueterate affect
Is euer full of anguish and defect. (Sig. I2r).

been gelded! I should then have been a fat fool for a
chamber, a squeaking fool for a tavern, and a private fool for   5
all the ladies.

MALEVOLE
You are in good case since you came to court, fool; what,
guarded, guarded!

PASSARELLO
Yes, faith, even as footmen and bawds wear velvet, not for
an ornament of honour, but for a badge of drudgery; for now   10
the duke is discontented I am fain to fool him asleep every
night.

MALEVOLE
What are his griefs?

PASSARELLO
He hath sore eyes.

MALEVOLE
I never observed so much.   15

PASSARELLO
Horrible sore eyes; and so hath every cuckold; for the roots
of the horns spring in the eyeballs, and that's the reason the
horn of a cuckold is as tender as his eye, or as that growing
in the woman's forehead twelve years since, that could not
endure to be touched. The duke hangs down his head like a   20
columbine.

MALEVOLE
Passarello, why do great men beg fools?

PASSARELLO
As the Welshman stole rushes when there was nothing else
to filch—only to keep begging in fashion.

MALEVOLE
Pooh! Thou givest no good reason; thou speakest like a fool.   25

PASSARELLO
Faith, I utter small fragments, as your knight courts your
city widow with jingling of his gilt spurs, advancing his

7 *in good case* well-dressed
8 *guarded* wearing facing or embroidery on his fool's coat
22 *beg fools* the king could grant custody of idiots, and the profits of
    their estates, to those who sued for them
27 *jingling . . . advancing* Q corrected (something of his guilt: some
    aduancing Q uncorrected)

18–20 *growing . . . touched.* Probably Margaret Griffith of Montgomery-
shire, described in a pamphlet of 1588 as having a four-inch horn in
the middle of her forehead.

bush-coloured beard, and taking tobacco. This is all the mirror
of their knightly complements. Nay, I shall talk when my
tongue is a-going once; 'tis like a citizen on horseback, ever-   30
more in a false gallop.

MALEVOLE

And how doth Maquerelle fare nowadays?

PASSARELLO

Faith, I was wont to salute her as our English women are at
their first landing in Flushing—I would call her whore; but
now that antiquity leaves her as an old piece of plastic t'work   35
by, I only ask her how her rotten teeth fare every morning,
and so leave her. She was the first that ever invented perfumed smocks for the gentlewomen, and woollen shoes for
fear of creaking, for the visitant. She were an excellent lady,
but that her face peeleth like Muscovy glass.   40

MALEVOLE

And how doth thy old lord that hath wit enough to be a
flatterer, and conscience enough to be a knave?

PASSARELLO

O excellent; he keeps, beside me, fifteen jesters to instruct
him in the art of fooling, and utters their jests in private to
the duke and duchess; he'll lie like to your Switzer or lawyer;   45
he'll be of any side for most money.

MALEVOLE

I am in haste, be brief.

PASSARELLO

As your fiddler when he is paid. He'll thrive, I warrant you,
while your young courtier stands like Good Friday in Lent—
men long to see it, because more fatting days come after it;   50
else he's the leanest and pitiful'st actor in the whole pageant.
Adieu, Malevole.

MALEVOLE

O world most vile, when thy loose vanities,
Taught by this fool, do make the fool seem wise!

PASSARELLO

You'll know me again, Malevole?   55

28 *bush-* Q corrected (high Q uncorrected)
29 *complements* accomplishments (also pun on book-title)
30–31 *citizen . . . gallop* lacking riding skill
34 *Flushing* the city was in English hands for several years after
   1585 as security for a loan from Elizabeth to the Dutch
35 *plastic* wax or clay model for sculpture
40 *Muscovy glass* mica or talc
41 *lord* i.e. Bilioso

MALEVOLE

O, ay, by that velvet.

PASSARELLO

Ay, as a pettifogger by his buckram bag. I am as common
in the court as an hostess's lips in the country; knights, and
clowns, and knaves, and all share me; the court cannot
possibly be without me. Adieu, Malevole.   *Exeunt*   60

Act II, Scene i

Enter MENDOZA *with a sconce, to observe* FERNEZE'S *entrance,
who, whilst the act is playing, enter[s] unbraced, two pages before
him with lights, is met by* MAQUERELLE, *and conveyed in. The
pages are sent away*

MENDOZA

He's caught! The woodcock's head is i' the noose.
Now treads Ferneze in dangerous path of lust,
Swearing his sense is merely deified.
The fool grasps clouds, and shall beget centaurs;
And now, in strength of panting faint delight,   5
The goat bids heaven envy him; good goose,
I can afford thee nothing
But the poor comfort of calamity, pity.
Lust's like the plummets hanging on clock lines,
Will ne'er ha' done, till all is quite undone.   10
Such is the course salt sallow lust doth run,
Which thou shalt try. I'll be revenged. Duke, thy suspect;
Duchess, thy disgrace; Ferneze, thy rivalship—
Shall have swift vengeance. Nothing so holy,
No band of nature so strong,   15
No law of friendship so sacred,
But I'll profane, burst, violate,
'Fore I'll endure disgrace, contempt and poverty.
Shall I, whose very 'hum' struck all heads bare,

57 *pettifogger* inferior lawyer, conducting petty cases
s.d. *sconce* lantern
      act . . . playing the music between the acts
      unbraced in undress
  1 *woodcock* dupe; woodcock were easily taken in snares
  3 *merely* completely
  4 *fool . . . centaurs* Ixion begat the Centaurs upon a cloud
  9 *plummets* weights
11 *salt* salacious
12 *suspect* suspicion

Whose face made silence, creaking of whose shoe   20
Forced the most private passages fly ope,
Scrape like a servile dog at some latched door?
Learn now to make a leg, and cry 'Beseech ye,
Pray ye, is such a lord within?'—be awed
At some odd usher's scoffed formality?   25
First sear my brains! *Unde cadis, non quo, refert.*
My heart cries 'Perish all!' How! how! What fate
Can once avoid revenge that's desperate?
I'll to the duke; if all should ope—if? tush!
Fortune still dotes on those who cannot blush.   *Exit*   30

Act II, Scene ii

Enter MALEVOLE *at one door,* BIANCA, EMILIA, *and* MAQUERELLE
at the other door

MALEVOLE

Bless ye, cast o' ladies. Ha, Dipsas! how dost thou, old coal?

MAQUERELLE

Old coal?

MALEVOLE

Ay, old coal; methinks thou liest like a brand under billets of
green wood. He that will inflame a young wench's heart,
let him lay close to her an old coal that hath first been fired, a   5
panderess, my half-burnt lint, who, though thou canst not
flame thyself, yet art able to set a thousand virgins' tapers
afire.—And how doth Janivere thy husband, my little peri-
winkle? Is he troubled with the cough o' the lungs still?
Does he hawk o' nights still? He will not bite.   10

23 *make a leg* bow
26 *sear* Q1, Q2 (seate Q)
   Unde . . . refert 'Whence you fall, not whither, matters' (based
   on Seneca, *Thyestes*, 925–6)
1 *cast* pair
   Dipsas! Q corrected (dip-sawce Q uncorrected)
3 *under billets* Q (under these billets Q1, Q2)   6 *lint* tinder
8 *Janivere* January (See Chaucer's *Merchant's Tale*)

1 *Dipsas.* The name is derived from a serpent whose bite caused un-
   quenchable thirst; it is also the name of a bawd in Ovid's *Amores*,
   I. viii, and of the enchantress in Lyly's *Endymion*; these allusions seem
   equally apt.
   old coal. 'A Maquerela, in plaine English a Bawde, Is an old char-cole,
   that hath been burnt her selfe, and therefore is able to kindle a whole
   greene coppice', Overbury's *Characters* (Bullen).

BIANCA

No, by my troth, I took him with his mouth empty of old
teeth.

MALEVOLE

And he took thee with thy belly full of young bones; marry,
he took his maim by the stroke of his enemy.

BIANCA

And I mine by the stroke of my friend.   15

MALEVOLE

The close stock! O mortal wench! Lady, ha' ye now no
restoratives for your decayed Jasons? Look ye, crab's guts
baked, distilled ox-pith, the pulverised hairs of a lion's
upper lip, jelly of cock-sparrows, he-monkey's marrow, or
powder of fox-stones? And whither are all you ambling now?   20

BIANCA

To bed, to bed.

MALEVOLE

Do your husbands lie with ye?

BIANCA

That were country-fashion, i' faith.

MALEVOLE

Ha' ye no foregoers about you? Come, whither in good deed,
la now?   25

MAQUERELLE

In good indeed, la now, to eat the most miraculously admir-
ably, astonishable-composed posset with three curds, without any drink. Will ye help me with a he-fox?—Here's the
duke.   *The ladies go out*

MALEVOLE

(*To* BIANCA) Fried frogs are very good, and French-like too.   30

Act II, Scene iii

Enter DUKE PIETRO, COUNT CELSO, COUNT EQUATO, BILIOSO,
FERRARDO, *and* MENDOZA

PIETRO

The night grows deep and foul; what hour is't?

16 *stock* stoccado, fencing thrust
17 *Jasons* Jason accomplished his tasks with the help of Medea's
   magic potions
17–20 *crab's . . . fox-stones* alleged aphrodisiacs
20 *powder* Q1, Q2 (powlder Q)
   are all you Q1, Q2 (are you Q)
23 *country-fashion* bawdy, as Hamlet to Ophelia

CELSO
Upon the stroke of twelve.

MALEVOLE
Save ye, duke.

PIETRO
From thee—Begone, I do not love thee! Let me see thee no
more, we are displeased. 5

MALEVOLE
Why, God be with thee! Heaven hear my curse—may thy
wife and thee live long together.

PIETRO
Begone, sirrah.

MALEVOLE
'When Arthur first in court began'—Agamemnon, Menelaus
—was ever any duke a cornuto? 10

PIETRO
Begone, hence.

MALEVOLE
What religion wilt thou be of next?

MENDOZA
Out with him!

MALEVOLE
With most servile patience—Time will come
When wonder of thy error will strike dumb 15
Thy bezzled sense.
Slaves i' favour! Ay, marry, shall he rise?
Good God! how subtle hell doth flatter vice,
Mounts him aloft, and makes him seem to fly;
As fowl the tortoise mocked, who to the sky 20
Th'ambitious shellfish raised. Th'end of all
Is only that from height he might dead fall.

BILIOSO
Why, when? Out ye rogue! Begone, ye rascal!

MALEVOLE
I shall now leave ye with all my best wishes.

BILIOSO
Out, ye cur! 25

---

9 'When . . . began' opening line of ballad (See 2 Henry IV, II. iv)
   Agamemnon—Menelaus cuckolded princes, like King Arthur
16 bezzled befuddled
17 Slaves i' favour Wine (slaues I fauour, I mary shall he, rise, Qq)
20–1 fowl . . . raised See Aesop's fable of the tortoise and the eagle
   (Aesop, ed. Halm, No. 419)

MALEVOLE
Only let's hold together a firm correspondence.
BILIOSO
Out!
MALEVOLE
A mutual, friendly-reciprocal, perpetual kind of steady-
unanimous-heartily-leagued—
BILIOSO
Hence, ye gross-jawed peasantly—out, go!   30
MALEVOLE
Adieu, pigeon-house! Thou burr that only stickest to nappy
fortunes; the serpigo, the strangury, an eternal, uneffectual
priapism seize thee!
BILIOSO
Out, rogue!
MALEVOLE
May'st thou be a notorious wittoly pander to thine own wife,   35
and yet get no office, but live to be the utmost misery of
mankind, a beggarly cuckold.   *Exit*
PIETRO
It shall be so.
MENDOZA
It must be so, for where great states revenge
'Tis requisite the parts which piety   40
And loft respect forbears be closely dogged.
Lay one into his breast shall sleep with him,
Feed in the same dish, run in self-faction,
Who may discover any shape of danger;
For once disgraced, displayèd in offence,   45

31 *nappy* rough
32 *serpigo* creeping skin disease, ringworm
   strangury bladder disability, causing painful urination
33 *priapism* penis erection
39 *states* statesmen
40 *parts* factions
   which ed. (with Qq)
41 *loft* Q, Q2 (soft Q1)
44 *discover* Q, Q2 (dissuer Q1)
45 *displayèd* Q, Q2 (discouered Q1)

39–41 *It . . . dogged.* Mendoza's advice is obscurely phrased; the required
   sense would seem to be that great men should set close watch upon
   those factious subjects who withhold due loyalty and respect: Aurelia
   is here the subject of the conversation, and her behaviour seems a
   clue to the thinking.

It makes man blushless, and man is (all confess)
More prone to vengeance than to gratefulness.
Favours are writ in dust, but stripes we feel,
Depraved nature stamps in lasting steel.

PIETRO

You shall be leagued with the duchess!   50

EQUATO

The plot is very good.

MENDOZA

You shall both kill, and seem the corse to save.

FERRARDO

A most fine brain-trick.

CELSO

(*Tacite*) Of a most cunning knave.

PIETRO

My lords, the heavy action we intend   55
Is death and shame, two of the ugliest shapes
That can confound a soul; think, think of it.
I strike, but yet like him that 'gainst stone walls
Directs his shafts, rebounds in his own face;
My lady's shame is mine; O God, 'tis mine!   60
Therefore I do conjure all secrecy;
Let it be as very little as may be—
Pray ye, as may be.
Make frightless entrance, salute her with soft eyes,
Stain naught with blood—only Ferneze dies,   65
But not before her brows. O gentlemen,
God knows I love her! Nothing else, but this—
I am not well. If grief, that sucks veins dry,
Rivels the skin, casts ashes in men's faces,
Bedulls the eye, unstrengthens all the blood,   70
Chance to remove me to another world,
As sure I once must die, let him succeed.
I have no child; all that my youth begot
Hath been your loves, which shall inherit me;
Which as it ever shall, I do conjure it,   75
Mendoza may succeed: he's noble born,
With me of much desert.

CELSO

(*Tacite*) Much!

54 (*Tacite*) silently, aside
61 *conjure* implore
65 *Stain* Q1 (Strain Q, Q2)
69 *Rivels* wrinkles   72 *him* i.e. Mendoza

PIETRO

Your silence answers 'Ay';
I thank you. Come on now. O that I might die   80
Before her shame's displayed! Would I were forced
To burn my father's tomb, unhele his bones,
And dash them in the dirt, rather than this!
This both the living and the dead offends;
Sharp surgery where naught but death amends.   85

                                        Exit with the others

Act II, Scene iv

Enter MAQUERELLE, EMILIA, *and* BIANCA, *with the posset*

MAQUERELLE

Even here it is; three curds in three regions individually
distinct; most methodical, according to art composed, without any drink.

BIANCA

Without any drink?

MAQUERELLE

Upon my honour; will you sit and eat?   5

EMILIA

Good—the composure, the receipt, how is't?

MAQUERELLE

'Tis a pretty pearl; by this pearl (how dost with me?) thus
it is: seven and thirty yolks of Barbary hens' eggs, eighteen
spoonfuls and a half of the juice of cocksparrow bones, one
ounce, three drams, four scruples, and one quarter of the   10
syrup of Ethiopian dates, sweetened with three-quarters of
a pound of pure candied Indian eringoes; strewed over with
the powder of pearl of America, amber of Cataia, and lamb-
stones of Muscovia.

BIANCA

Trust me, the ingredients are very cordial, and no question   15
good, and most powerful in restoration.

82 *unhele* strip off covering (vnheale Q; vnhill Q1, Q2)
   1–2 *three . . . distinct* junkets of curds and similar dishes are
        composed in layers, usually sweet and sour
   6 *composure* composition
   7 *pearl* Emilia has to buy the information
        (*how . . . me?*) 'how does it become me?' (Neilson)
   12 *eringoes* roots of sea holly
   13 *Cataia* Cathay (China)
   13–14 *lamb-stones* lamb's fry   15 *cordial* invigorating

MAQUERELLE
I know not what you mean by restoration, but this it doth:
it purifieth the blood, smootheth the skin, enliveneth the eye,
strengtheneth the veins, mundifieth the teeth, comforteth the
stomach, fortifieth the back, and quickeneth the wit; that's   20
all.

EMILIA
By my troth, I have eaten but two spoonfuls, and methinks
I could discourse most swiftly and wittily already.

MAQUERELLE
Have you the art to seem honest?

BIANCA
Ay, thank advice and practice.   25

MAQUERELLE
Why then, eat me of this posset, quicken your blood, and
preserve your beauty. Do you know Doctor Plaster-face? By
this curd, he is the most exquisite in forging of veins,
sprightening of eyes, dyeing of hair, sleeking of skins,
blushing of cheeks, surphling of breasts, blanching and   30
bleaching of teeth, that ever made an old lady gracious by
torchlight; by this curd, la.

BIANCA
We are resolved, what God has given us we'll cherish.

MAQUERELLE
Cherish anything saving your husband; keep him not too
high lest he leap the pale. But for your beauty, let it be your
saint, bequeath two hours to it every morning in your closet.
I ha' been young, and yet in my conscience I am not above
five and twenty, but believe me, preserve and use your
beauty, for youth and beauty once gone, we are like beehives
without honey, out o' fashion apparel that no man will wear;   40
therefore, use me your beauty.

EMILIA
Ay, but men say—

MAQUERELLE
Men say? Let men say what they will; life o' woman, they are

19 *mundifieth* cleans
29 *sprightening* making vivacious
30 *surphling* washing with sulphur water or other cosmetics
34–5 *keep . . . pale* the spirited beast will leap the fence; also bawdy
41 *use* put to use

24–49 *Have . . . beauties.* See Introduction, p. xxvi.

ignorant of your wants. The more in years, the more in per-
fection they grow; if they lose youth and beauty, they gain   45
wisdom and discretion. But when our beauty fades, goodnight with us. There cannot be an uglier thing to see than
an old woman; from which, O pruning, pinching, and painting, deliver all sweet beauties.

BIANCA
Hark! Music.   50

MAQUERELLE
Peace, 'tis the duchess' bed-chamber. Good rest, most
prosperously-graced ladies.

EMILIA
Good night, sentinel.

BIANCA
'Night, dear Maquerelle.   *Exeunt all but* MAQUERELLE

MAQUERELLE
May my posset's operation send you my wit and honesty,   55
and me your youth and beauty: the pleasing'st rest.

Exit MAQUERELLE

Act II, Scene v

A song

Whilst the song is singing, enter MENDOZA *with his sword drawn.*
standing ready to murder FERNEZE *as he flies from the duchess'*
chamber

ALL
[*Within*] Strike, strike!

AURELIA
[*Within*] Save my Ferneze! O save my Ferneze!

Enter FERNEZE *in his shirt, and is received upon* MENDOZA'S
sword

ALL
[*Within*] Follow! Pursue!

AURELIA
[*Within*] O save Ferneze!

[MENDOZA] *thrusts his rapier in* FERNEZE

MENDOZA
Pierce, pierce! Thou shallow fool, drop there.   5

44 *your* Q (our Q1, Q2)
5 *s.d.* Wine (after l. 8 Q, Q2; not in Q1)

He that attempts a princess' lawless love
Must have broad hands, close heart, with Argus' eyes,
And back of Hercules; or else he dies.

Enter AURELIA, DUKE PIETRO, FERRARDO, BILIOSO, CELSO, *and*
EQUATO

ALL
Follow, follow!
MENDOZA
Stand off, forbear, ye most uncivil lords!   10
PIETRO
Strike!
MENDOZA
Do not. Tempt not a man resolved.

MENDOZA *bestrides the wounded body of* FERNEZE *and seems to
save him*

Would you, inhuman murderers, more than death?
AURELIA
O poor Ferneze!
MENDOZA
Alas, now all defence too late.
AURELIA
                                        He's dead.   15
PIETRO
I am sorry for our shame. Go to your bed.
Weep not too much, but leave some tears to shed
When I am dead.
AURELIA
What, weep for thee? My soul no tears shall find.
PIETRO
Alas, alas, that women's souls are blind.   20
MENDOZA
Betray such beauty?
Murder such youth? Contemn civility?
He loves him not that rails not at him.
PIETRO
Thou canst not move us; we have blood enough;
And please you, lady, we have quite forgot   25
All your defects; if not, why then—

7 *Argus* Argos Panoptes had eyes all over his body
8 *Hercules* See IV. v, ll. 58–9
12 *s.d.* Q1, Q2 (not in Q)

AURELIA
  Not.
PIETRO
  Not. The best of rest, good night.

Exit PIETRO *with other courtiers*

AURELIA
  Despite go with thee!
MENDOZA
  Madam, you ha' done me foul disgrace; you have wronged   30
  him much loves you too much. Go to, your soul knows you
  have.
AURELIA
  I think I have.
MENDOZA
  Do you but think so?
AURELIA
  Nay, sure, I have; my eyes have witnessed thy love; thou   35
  hast stood too firm for me.
MENDOZA
  Why, tell me, fair-cheeked lady, who even in tears art
  powerfully beauteous, what unadvised passion struck ye
  into such a violent heat against me? Speak; what mischief
  wronged us? What devil injured us? Speak.   40
AURELIA
  That thing ne'er worthy of the name of man—Ferneze.
  Ferneze swore thou lov'st Emilia,
  Which, to advance, with most reproachful breath
  Thou both didst blemish and denounce my love.
MENDOZA
  Ignoble villain, did I for this bestride   45
  Thy wounded limbs? For this, rank opposite
  Even to my sovereign? O God, for this,
  Sunk all my hopes, and with my hopes, my life?
  Ripped bare my throat unto the hangman's axe?
  Thou most dishonoured trunk! Emilia?   50
  By life, I know her not—Emilia?
  Did you believe him?
AURELIA   Pardon me, I did.
MENDOZA
  Did you? And thereupon you graced him?
AURELIA
  I did.

46 *rank* take stand
46–7 *For . . . sovereign?* Q1, Q2 (not in Q)

MENDOZA
  Took him to favour, nay, even clasped with him?   55
AURELIA
  Alas, I did.
MENDOZA
  This night?
AURELIA
  This night.
MENDOZA
  And in your lustful twines the duke took you?
AURELIA
  A most sad truth.   60
MENDOZA
  O God! O God! how we dull honest souls,
  Heavy-brained men, are swallowed in the bogs
  Of a deceitful ground, whilst nimble bloods,
  Light-jointed spirits, pent, cut good men's throats,
  And scape. Alas, I am too honest for this age,   65
  Too full of phlegm and heavy steadiness;
  Stood still whilst this slave cast a noose about me:
  Nay, then to stand in honour of him and her
  Who had even sliced my heart!
AURELIA
  Come; I did err, and am most sorry I did err.   70
MENDOZA
  Why, we are both but dead; the duke hates us;
  And those whom princes do once groundly hate,
  Let them provide to die; as sure as fate,
  Prevention is the heart of policy.
AURELIA
  Shall we murder him?   75
MENDOZA
  Instantly?
AURELIA
  Instantly; before he casts a plot,
  Or further blaze my honour's much-known blot.
  Let's murder him.
MENDOZA
  I would do much for you; will ye marry me?   80

64 *pent* Q1, Q2 (spent Q)
72 *groundly* thoroughly
73 *provide* make ready
74 *Prevention* anticipation
78 *blaze* proclaim

AURELIA

I'll make thee duke. We are of Medicis,
Florence our friend; in court my faction
Not meanly strengthful; the duke then dead,
We well-prepared for change; the multitude
Irresolutely reeling; we in force;   85
Our party seconded; the kingdom mazed;
No doubt of swift success all shall be graced.

MENDOZA

You do confirm me, we are resolute;
Tomorrow look for change; rest confident.
'Tis now about the immodest waist of night;   90
The mother of moist dew with pallid light
Spreads gloomy shades about the numbèd earth.
Sleep, sleep, whilst we contrive our mischief's birth.
This man I'll get inhumed. Farewell; to bed;
Ay kiss thy pillow, dream, the duke is dead.   *Exit* AURELIA   95
So, so, good night. How fortune dotes on impudence! I am
in private the adopted son of yon good prince. I must be
duke. Why, if I must, I must. Most silly lord, name me? O
heaven! I see God made honest fools to maintain crafty
knaves. The duchess is wholly mine too; must kill her   100
husband to quit her shame—much! then marry her. Ay, O
I grow proud in prosperous treachery!
As wrestlers clip, so I'll embrace you all,
Not to support, but to procure your fall.

Enter MALEVOLE

MALEVOLE

God arrest thee.   105

MENDOZA

At whose suit?

MALEVOLE

At the devil's. Ah, you treacherous, damnable monster! How
dost? How dost, thou treacherous rogue? Ah ye rascal, I am
banished the court, sirrah.

MENDOZA

Prithee, let's be acquainted; I do love thee, faith.   110

MALEVOLE

At your service, by the Lord, la! Shall's go to supper? Let's

86 *mazed* confused
87 *of* by means of
94 *inhumed* buried
95 *kiss thy* Q1, Q2 (kiss the Q)   98 *silly* Q1, Q2 (seely Q)

be once drunk together, and so unite a most virtuously
strengthened friendship; shall's, Huguenot, shall's?

MENDOZA
Wilt fall upon my chamber tomorrow morn?

MALEVOLE
As a raven to a dunghill. They say there's one dead here,   115
pricked for the pride of the flesh.

MENDOZA
Ferneze. There he is; prithee, bury him.

MALEVOLE
O most willingly; I mean to turn pure Rochelle churchman, I.

MENDOZA
Thou churchman? Why? Why?

MALEVOLE
Because I'll live lazily, rail upon authority, deny kings'   120
supremacy in things indifferent, and be a pope in mine own
parish.

MENDOZA
Wherefore dost thou think churches were made?

MALEVOLE
To scour ploughshares; I ha' seen oxen plough up altars.
Et nunc seges ubi Sion fuit.   125

MENDOZA
Strange.

MALEVOLE
Nay, monstrous! I ha' seen a sumptuous steeple turned to a
stinking privy; more beastly, the sacredest place made a dog's
kennel; nay, most inhuman, the stoned coffins of long-dead
Christians burst up and made hogs' troughs. *Hic finis Priami.* 130
Shall I ha' some sack and cheese at thy chamber? Good night,
good mischievous incarnate devil, good night, Mendoza.
Ah, you inhuman villain, good night; 'night, fub.

MENDOZA
Good night; tomorrow morn.   *Exit* MENDOZA

MALEVOLE
Ay, I will come, friendly damnation, I will come. I do descry 135

113 *Huguenot* confederate (Fr. Hugues; Ger. eidgenoss)
118 *Rochelle churchman* La Rochelle was a centre of relief for
    Huguenots during periods of persecution
125 *et nunc . . . fuit* 'And now corn grows where Sion was' (based on
    'Jam seges est ubi Troja fuit', Ovid, *Heroides*, l. 53)
130 *Hic finis Priami* 'Here was Priam's end' (based on 'Haec finis
    Priami fatorum', Virgil, *Aeneid* II, l. 554)
133 *fub* cheat

cross-points; honesty and courtship straddle as far asunder
as a true Frenchman's legs.

FERNEZE

O!

MALEVOLE

Proclamations, more proclamations!

FERNEZE

O, a surgeon!   140

MALEVOLE

Hark! Lust cries for a surgeon; what news from limbo? How
does the grand cuckold, Lucifer?

FERNEZE

O help, help! Conceal and save me.

FERNEZE *stirs, and* MALEVOLE *helps him up, and conveys him
away*

MALEVOLE

Thy shame more than thy wounds do grieve me far;
Thy wounds but leave upon thy flesh some scar;   145
But fame ne'er heals, still rankles worse and worse;
Such is of uncontrollèd lust the curse.
Think what it is in lawless sheets to lie;
But, O, Ferneze, what in lust to die.
Then thou that shame respects, O, fly converse   150
With women's eyes and lisping wantonness.
Stick candles 'gainst a virgin wall's white back,
If they not burn, yet at the least they'll black.
Come, I'll convey thee to a private port,
Where thou shalt live (O happy man) from court.   155
The beauty of the day begins to rise,
From whose bright form night's heavy shadow flies.
Now 'gins close plots to work, the scene grows full,
And craves his eyes who hath a solid skull.   *Exeunt*

Act III, Scene i

Enter DUKE PIETRO, MENDOZA, COUNT EQUATO *and* BILIOSO

PIETRO

'Tis grown to youth of day; how shall we waste this light?
My heart's more heavy than a tyrant's crown. Shall we go
hunt? Prepare for field.   *Exit* EQUATO

136 *cross-points* tricks (pun on dancing term)
142 *does* Q1, Q2 (doth Q)   146 *fame* ill report
154 *port* place of refuge   155 *from* away from

MENDOZA
  Would ye could be merry.
PIETRO
  Would God I could! Mendoza, bid 'em haste. *Exit* MENDOZA   5
  I would fain shift place. O vain relief!
  Sad souls may well change place, but not change grief;
  As deer, being struck, fly thorough many soils,
  Yet still the shaft sticks fast, so—
BILIOSO
  A good old simile, my honest lord.   10
PIETRO
  I am not much unlike to some sick man
  That long desired hurtful drink; at last
  Swills in and drinks his last, ending at once
  Both life and thirst. O would I ne'er had known
  My own dishonour! Good God, that men should desire   15
  To search out that, which being found, kills all
  Their joy of life! To taste the tree of knowledge,
  And then be driven from out paradise.
  Canst give me some comfort?
BILIOSO
  My lord, I have some books which have been dedicated to   20
  my honour, and I ne'er read 'em, and yet they had very fine
  names: *Physic for Fortune, Lozenges of Sanctified Sincerity*,
  very pretty works of curates, scriveners, and schoolmasters.
  Marry, I remember one Seneca, Lucius Annaeus Seneca—
PIETRO
  Out upon him! He writ of temperance and fortitude, yet   25
  lived like a voluptuous epicure, and died like an effeminate
  coward. Haste thee to Florence.
  Here, take our letters, see 'em sealed; away.
  Report in private to the honoured duke
  His daughter's forced disgrace; tell him at length   30
  We know too much; due compliments advance.
  There's naught that's safe and sweet but ignorance.
                                        Exit DUKE
                   Enter BIANCA
BILIOSO
  Madam, I am going ambassador for Florence; 'twill be great
  charges to me.

8 *soils* stretches of water in which hunted animals try to lose scent
34 *charges* expense
_____

22 *Physic for Fortune.* Petrarch's *De Remediis Utriusque Fortunae* (1386)
  was translated by Thomas Twyne as *Physicke against Fortune* (1579).

BIANCA

No matter, my lord, you have the lease of two manors come   35
out next Christmas; you may lay your tenants on the greater
rack for it; and when you come home again, I'll teach you
how you shall get two hundred pounds a year by your teeth.

BILIOSO

How, madam?

BIANCA

Cut off so much from housekeeping; that which is saved by   40
the teeth, you know, is got by the teeth.

BILIOSO

'Fore God, and so I may; I am in wondrous credit, lady.

BIANCA

See the use of flattery; I did ever counsel you to flatter
greatness, and you have profited well. Any man that will do
so shall be sure to be like your Scotch barnacle—now a   45
block, instantly a worm, and presently a great goose. This it
is to rot and putrefy in the bosom of greatness.

BILIOSO

Thou art ever my politician. O, how happy is that old lord
that hath a politician to his young lady! I'll have fifty gentlemen shall attend upon me; marry, the most of them shall be   50
farmers' sons, because they shall bear their own charges;
and they shall go apparelled thus, in sea-water-green suits,
ash-colour cloaks, watchet stockings, and popinjay-green
feathers—will not the colours do excellent?

BIANCA

Out upon't! They'll look like citizens riding to their friends   55
at Whitsuntide, their apparel just so many several parishes.

BILIOSO

I'll have it so; and Passarello, my fool, shall go along with
me; marry, he shall be in velvet.

BIANCA

A fool in velvet?

BILIOSO

Ay, 'tis common for your fool to wear satin; I'll have mine   60
in velvet.

BIANCA

What will you wear then, my lord?

35–6 *come out* expire
42 *credit* reputation   53 *watchet* light blue

---

45 *Scotch barnacle.* An account 'Of the Goose tree, Barnacle tree, or the
tree bearing Geese' is in Gerard's *Herball* (1597), Chap. 188.

BILIOSO

Velvet too; marry, it shall be embroidered, because I'll differ
from the fool somewhat. I am horribly troubled with the
gout; nothing grieves me but that my doctor hath forbidden   65
me wine, and you know your ambassador must drink. Didst
thou ask thy doctor what was good for the gout?

BIANCA

Yes; he said ease, wine and women were good for it.

BILIOSO

Nay, thou hast such a wit. What was good to cure it, said he?

BIANCA

Why, the rack; all your empirics could never do the like cure   70
upon the gout the rack did in England, or your Scotch boot.
The French harlequin will instruct you.

BILIOSO

Surely, I do wonder how thou, having for the most part of
thy lifetime been a country body, shouldst have so good a
wit.   75

BIANCA

Who, I? Why, I have been a courtier thrice two months.

BILIOSO

So have I this twenty year, and yet there was a gentleman-
usher called me coxcomb t'other day, and to my face too.
Was't not a backbiting rascal? I would I were better travelled,
that I might have been better acquainted with the fashions of   80
several countrymen; but my secretary, I think he hath suffici-
ently instructed me.

BIANCA

How, my lord?

BILIOSO

'Marry, my good lord', quoth he, 'your lordship shall ever
find amongst a hundred Frenchmen, forty hot-shots;   85
amongst a hundred Spaniards, threescore braggarts; amongst
a hundred Dutchmen, fourscore drunkards; amongst a
hundred Englishmen, fourscore and ten madmen; and
amongst a hundred Welshmen—'

BIANCA

What, my lord?   90

70 *empirics* sect of empirical physicians
71 *Scotch boot* instrument of torture by which legs were crushed
72 *harlequin* (Herlakeene Q) referred to probably because the Scotch
    boot was used in Scotland and France
81 *several countrymen* of several countries

BILIOSO

'Fourscore and nineteen gentlemen.'

BIANCA

But since you go about a sad embassy, I would have you go in black, my lord.

BILIOSO

Why, dost think I cannot mourn unless I wear my hat in cypress like an alderman's heir? That's vile, very old, in   95 faith.

BIANCA

I'll learn of you shortly. O we should have a fine gallant of you, should not I instruct you. How will you bear yourself when you come into the Duke of Florence' court?

BILIOSO

Proud enough, and 'twill do well enough. As I walk up and   100 down the chamber I'll spit frowns about me, have a strong perfume in my jerkin, let my beard grow to make me look terrible, salute no man beneath the fourth button, and 'twill do excellent.

BIANCA

But there is a very beautiful lady there; how will you enter-   105 tain her?

BILIOSO

I'll tell you that when the lady hath entertained me. But to satisfy thee, here comes the fool.

Enter PASSARELLO

Fool, thou shalt stand for the fair lady.

PASSARELLO

Your fool will stand for your lady most willingly and most   110 uprightly.

BILIOSO

I'll salute her in Latin.

PASSARELLO

O, your fool can understand no Latin.

BILIOSO

Ay, but your lady can.

PASSARELLO

Why then, if your lady take down your fool, your fool will   115 stand no longer for your lady.

91 *gentlemen* Welshmen were proverbially proud of their pedigrees
95 *cypress* light, transparent material of silk and linen, used for veiling
103 *salute . . . button* make no low bows

BILIOSO

A pestilent fool! 'Fore God, I think the world be turned
upside down too.

PASSARELLO

O no, sir; for then your lady, and all the ladies in the palace,
should go with their heels upward, and that were a strange   120
sight you know.

BILIOSO

There be many will repine at my preferment.

PASSARELLO

O ay, like the envy of an elder sister that hath her younger
made a lady before her.

BILIOSO

The duke is wondrous discontented.   125

PASSARELLO

Ay, and more melancholic than a usurer having all his money
out at the death of a prince.

BILIOSO

Didst thou see Madam Floria today?

PASSARELLO

Yes, I found her repairing her face today; the red upon the
white showed as if her cheeks should have been served in for   130
two dishes of barberries in stewed broth, and the flesh to
them a woodcock.

BILIOSO

A bitter fool! Come, madam, this night thou shalt enjoy me
freely, and tomorrow for Florence.

> [*Walks* BIANCA *aside: exit* BIANCA]

PASSARELLO

What a natural fool is he that would be a pair of bodies to a   135
woman's petticoat, to be trussed and pointed to them. Well,
I'll dog my lord, and the word is proper; for when I fawn
upon him he feeds me; when I snap him by the fingers, he
spits in my mouth. If a dog's death were not strangling, I
had rather be one than a serving-man; for the corruption of   140
coin is either the generation of a usurer, or a lousy beggar.

> [*Exit*]

122 *preferment* advancement
131 *barberries* Barbary hens
133 *fool* punning on fowl, carried on through 'trussed and pointed'
    below
135 *bodies* punning on bodice
136 *trussed and pointed* tied with points (laces)

Act III, Scene ii

Enter MALEVOLE *in some frieze gown, whilst* BILIOSO *reads his patent*

MALEVOLE

    I cannot sleep; my eyes' ill-neighbouring lids
    Will hold no fellowship. O thou pale sober night,
    Thou that in sluggish fumes all sense doth steep,
    Thou that gives all the world full leave to play,
    Unbend'st the feebled veins of sweaty labour.   5
    The galley-slave, that all the toilsome day
    Tugs at his oar against the stubborn wave,
    Straining his rugged veins, snores fast;
    The stooping scythe-man that doth barb the field
    Thou mak'st wink sure. In night all creatures sleep;   10
    Only the malcontent, that 'gainst his fate
    Repines and quarrels—alas, he's goodman tell-clock;
    His sallow jaw-bones sink with wasting moan;
    Whilst others' beds are down, his pillow's stone.

BILIOSO

    Malevole.   15

MALEVOLE

    Elder of Israel, thou honest defect of wicked nature and
    obstinate ignorance, when did thy wife let thee lie with her?

BILIOSO

    I am going ambassador to Florence.

MALEVOLE

    Ambassador? Now, for thy country's honour, prithee do
    not put up mutton and porridge in thy cloak-bag. Thy young   20
    lady wife goes to Florence with thee too, does she not?

BILIOSO

    No, I leave her at the palace.

MALEVOLE

    At the palace? Now discretion shield man! For God's love,

s.d. *frieze* woollen cloth with heavy nap
    patent commission as ambassador
  9 *barb* mow
 12 *tell-clock* calling the hours of night watches
 16 *Elder of Israel* wicked old judge (Harrier cites Thomas Nashe,
    Pierce Penilesse: Works ed. McKerrow and Wilson, I, p. 188)

---

 16 *thou . . . nature.* Cf. *Il pastor fido*, II. vi:

      'Dryed *Carogne*, defect of wicked nature' (Sig. G)

    (*Carogne*＝carrion).

let's ha' no more cuckolds. Hymen begins to put off his
saffron robe. Keep thy wife i' the state of grace. Heart   25
o' truth, I would sooner leave my lady singled in a bordello
than in the Genoa palace.
Sin there appearing in her sluttish shape,
Would soon grow loathsome, even to blushes' sense;
Surfeit would choke intemperate appetite,   30
Make the soul scent the rotten breath of lust.
When in an Italian lascivious palace,
A lady guardianless,
Left to the push of all allurement,
The strongest incitements to immodesty,   35
To have her bound, incensed with wanton sweets,
Her veins filled high with heating delicates,
Soft rest, sweet music, amorous masquerers,
Lascivious banquets, sin itself gilt o'er,
Strong fantasy tricking up strange delights,   40
Presenting it dressed pleasingly to sense,
Sense leading it unto the soul, confirmed
With potent example, impudent custom,
Enticed by that great bawd, Opportunity;
Thus being prepared, clap to her easy ear   45
Youth in good clothes, well-shaped, rich,
Fair-spoken, promising-noble, ardent, blood-full,
Witty, flattering—Ulysses absent,
O Ithaca, can chastest Penelope hold out?

BILIOSO
Mass, I'll think on't; farewell.   *Exit* BILIOSO   50

MALEVOLE
Farewell; take thy wife with thee; farewell.
To Florence, um? It may prove good, it may;
And we may once unmask our brows.

24–5 *Hymen . . . robe* god of marriage, usually dressed in saffron robe
     in dramatic representations; Bilioso imperils his marriage by
     going abroad without his wife
26 *singled* alone
   bordello brothel
28 *there* in the bordello
30 *choke* ed. (cloke Q)   37 *delicates* delicacies
44 *Opportunity* often so described (See *The Rape of Lucrece*, l. 886)
49 *Ithaca, can chastest* Q1, Q2 (Ithacan, chastest Q.)

40–4 *Strong . . . Opportunity.* For Marston's use of these terms, and their
     indebtedness to Epictetus, see Davenport, pp. 346–7; the vocabulary
     is used again at III. iii, 72–5.

Act III, Scene iii

Enter COUNT CELSO

CELSO
My honoured lord.

MALEVOLE
Celso, peace! How is't? Speak low, pale fears
Suspect that hedges, walls and trees have ears.
Speak, how runs all?

CELSO
I' faith, my lord, that beast with many heads,   5
The staggering multitude, recoils apace;
Though thorough great men's envy, most men's malice,
Their much intemperate heat hath banished you,
Yet now they find envy and malice ne'er
Produce faint reformation.   10
The duke, the too soft duke, lies as a block,
For which two tugging factions seem to saw,
But still the iron through the ribs they draw.

MALEVOLE
I tell thee, Celso, I have ever found
Thy breast most far from shifting cowardice   15
And fearful baseness: therefore, I'll tell thee, Celso,
I find the wind begins to come about;
I'll shift my suit of fortune.
I know the Florentine—whose only force,
By marrying his proud daughter to this prince,   20
Both banished me, and made this weak lord duke—
Will now forsake them all, be sure he will.
I'll lie in ambush for conveniency,
Upon their severance to confirm myself.

CELSO
Is Ferneze interred?   25

MALEVOLE
Of that at leisure; he lives.

CELSO
But how stands Mendoza? How is't with him?

MALEVOLE
Faith, like a pair of snuffers; snibs filth in other men and
retains it in himself.

19 *only force* power alone
24 *confirm* strengthen
28 *snibs* snubs, reproves   29 *himself* Q1, Q2 (itself Q)

CELSO

 He does fly from public notice, methinks, as a hare does 30
 from hounds; the feet whereon he flies betrays him.

MALEVOLE

 I can track him, Celso.
 O, my disguise fools him most powerfully;
 For that I seem a desperate malcontent
 He fain would clasp with me; he is the true slave 35
 That will put on the most affected grace
 For some vile second cause.

Enter MENDOZA

CELSO   He's here.

MALEVOLE   Give place.

                Exit CELSO

 Illo, ho, ho, ho! Art there, old truepenny? Where hast thou
 spent thyself this morning? I see flattery in thine eyes and
 damnation in thy soul. Ha, thou huge rascal! 40

MENDOZA

 Thou art very merry.

MALEVOLE

 As a scholar *futuens gratis*. How doth the devil go with thee
 now?

MENDOZA

 Malevole, thou art an arrant knave.

MALEVOLE

 Who I? I have been a sergeant, man. 45

MENDOZA

 Thou art very poor.

MALEVOLE

 As Job, an alchemist, or a poet.

MENDOZA

 The duke hates thee.

MALEVOLE

 As Irishmen do bum-cracks.

MENDOZA

 Thou hast lost his amity. 50

MALEVOLE

 As pleasing as maids lose their virginity.

42 *futuens gratis* 'fornicating free' (Harrier cites Seneca, *Epistle*
 XLIV, quoting Plato)
45 *sergeant* sheriff's officer
49 *As . . . cracks* Irish objections to wind-breaking seem proverbial
 (Harrier cites Nashe, *ed. cit.* same page)

MENDOZA

Would thou wert of a lusty spirit; would thou wert noble.

MALEVOLE

Why, sure my blood gives me I am noble; sure I am of noble
kind, for I find myself possessed with all their qualities;
love dogs, dice and drabs, scorn wit in stuff-clothes, have   55
beat my shoemaker, knocked my seamstress, cuckold[ed]
my pothecary, and undone my tailor. Noble? Why not?
Since the Stoic said, *Neminem servum non ex regibus, neminem
regem non ex servis esse oriundum*—only busy Fortune touses,
and the provident Chances blends them together. I'll give   60
you a simile; did you e'er see a well with two buckets?
Whilst one comes up full to be emptied, another goes down
empty to be filled; such is the state of all humanity. Why,
look you, I may be the son of some duke; for, believe me,
intemperate lascivious bastardy makes nobility doubtful. I   65
have a lusty daring heart, Mendoza.

MENDOZA

Let's grasp! I do like thee infinitely. Wilt enact one thing
for me?

MALEVOLE

Shall I get by it? ([MENDOZA] *gives him his purse*) Command
me; I am thy slave beyond death and hell.   70

MENDOZA

Murder the duke.

MALEVOLE

My heart's wish, my soul's desire, my fantasy's dream, my
blood's longing, the only height of my hopes! How, O God,
how? O how my united spirits throng together, so strengthen
my resolve!   75

MENDOZA

The duke is now a-hunting.

MALEVOLE

Excellent, admirable, as the devil would have it! Lend me,
lend me rapier, pistol, cross-bow; so, so, I'll do it.

MENDOZA

Then we agree?

53 *gives* shows
55 *drabs* whores   *stuff-clothes* coarse cloth garments
58–9 *Neminem . . . oriundum* 'There is no slave not born of kings,
no king not born of slaves' (Seneca, *Epistle* XLIV, again quoting
Plato)
59 *only* alone   *touses* puts in disorder
67 *grasp* embrace   69 *get* gain

MALEVOLE

As Lent and fishmongers. Come, *a-cap-a-pe*, how? Inform.   80

MENDOZA

Know that this weak-brain'd duke, who only stands on
Florence' stilts, hath out of witless zeal made me his heir, and
secretly confirmed the wreath to me after his life's full point.

MALEVOLE

Upon what merit?

MENDOZA

Merit! By heaven, I horn him; only Ferneze's death gave me   85
state's life.

Tut, we are politic, he must not live now.

MALEVOLE

No reason, marry. But how must he die now?

MENDOZA

My utmost project is to murder the duke, that I might have
his estate, because he makes me his heir; to banish the
duchess, that I might be rid of a cunning Lacedaemonian,   90
because I know Florence will forsake her; and then to marry
Maria, the banished Duke Altofront's wife, that her friends
might strengthen me and my faction; this is all, la.

MALEVOLE

Do you love Maria?

MENDOZA

Faith, no great affection, but as wise men do love great   95
women, to ennoble their blood and augment their revenue.
To accomplish this now, thus now. The duke is in the forest
next the sea; single him, kill him, hurl him in the main, and
proclaim thou sawest wolves eat him.

MALEVOLE

Um; not so good. Methinks when he is slain, to get some   100
hypocrite, some dangerous wretch that's muffled o'er with
feigned holiness, to swear he heard the duke on some steep
cliff lament his wife's dishonour, and in an agony of his
heart's torture, hurled his groaning sides into the swollen
sea.—This circumstance well made sounds probable, and   105
hereupon the duchess—

MENDOZA

May well be banished. O unpeerable invention! Rare! Thou
god of policy! It honeys me.

80 *a-cap-a-pe* from head to foot   83 *point* end
90 *Lacedaemonian* slang for 'whore' (Spartan women had unaccus-
tomed equality with men)
107 *unpeerable* peerless

MALEVOLE

Then fear not for the wife of Altofront; I'll close to her.

MENDOZA

Thou shalt, thou shalt. Our excellency is pleased. Why wert   110
not thou an emperor? When we are duke I'll make thee some
great man sure.

MALEVOLE

Nay, make me some rich knave, and I'll make myself some
great man.

MENDOZA

In thee be all my spirit.   115
Retain ten souls, unite thy virtual powers;
Resolve; ha, remember greatness. Heart, farewell.

Enter CELSO

The fate of all my hopes in thee doth dwell. [*Exit* MENDOZA]

MALEVOLE

Celso, didst hear? O heaven, didst hear
Such devilish mischief? Sufferest thou the world   120
Carouse damnation even with greedy swallow,
And still dost wink, still does thy vengeance slumber?
If now thy brows are clear, when will they thunder?
                                                   [*Exeunt*]

Act III, Scene iv

Enter PIETRO, FERRARDO, PREPASSO, *and three* PAGES

FERRARDO

The dogs are at a fault.   *Cornets like horns*

PIETRO

Would God nothing but the dogs were at it! Let the deer
pursue safely, the dogs follow the game, and do you follow
the dogs. As for me, 'tis unfit one beast should hunt another.
I ha' one chaseth me. An't please you, I would be rid of ye a   5
little.

FERRARDO

Would your grief would as soon leave you as we to quietness.

PIETRO

I thank you.   *Exeunt* FERRARDO *and* PREPASSO
Boy, what dost thou dream of now?

109 *close to* come to terms with
116 *virtual* effective

PAGE

Of a dry summer, my lord, for here's a hot world towards.   10
But, my lord, I had a strange dream last night.

PIETRO

What strange dream?

PAGE

Why, methought I pleased you with singing, and then I
dreamed you gave me that short sword.

PIETRO

Prettily begged. Hold thee, I'll prove thy dream true; take't.   15

PAGE

My duty; but still I dreamed on, my lord, and methought,
and't shall please your excellency, you would needs out of
your royal bounty give me that jewel in your hat.

PIETRO

O, thou didst but dream, boy; do not believe it; dreams
prove not always true. They may hold in a short sword, but   20
not in a jewel. But now, sir, you dreamed you had pleased
me with singing; make that true as I have made the other.

PAGE

Faith, my lord, I did but dream; and dreams, you say,
prove not always true. They may hold in a good sword, but
not in a good song. The truth is, I ha' lost my voice.   25

PIETRO

Lost thy voice, how?

PAGE

With dreaming, faith. But here's a couple of sirenical rascals
shall enchant ye. What shall they sing, my good lord?

PIETRO

Sing of the nature of women, and then the song shall be
surely full of variety, old crotchets and most sweet closes;   30
it shall be humorous, grave, fantastic, amorous, melancholy,
sprightly, one in all, and all in one.

PAGE

All in one?

PIETRO

By'r lady, too many. Sing; my speech grows culpable of
unthrifty idleness; sing.   35

Song

10 *dry summer* to dream of a dry summer is proverbial
27 *sirenical* siren-like, alluring
30 *crotchets* quarter-notes; pun on whimsical fancies
  closes cadences; also bawdy   33 *All in one?* bawdy

Act III, Scene v

Enter MALEVOLE, *with cross-bow and pistol*

PIETRO

Ah, so, so; sing. I am heavy; walk off; I shall talk in my
sleep; walk off.   *Exeunt* PAGES

MALEVOLE

Brief, brief; who? The duke? Good heaven, that fools should
stumble upon greatness! Do not sleep, duke—give ye good
morrow. You must be brief, duke. I am fee'd to murder thee   5
—start not. Mendoza, Mendoza hired me; here's his gold,
his pistol, cross-bow and sword; 'tis all as firm as earth. O
fool, fool, choked with the common maze of easy idiots,
credulity! Make him thine heir? What, thy sworn murderer?

PIETRO

O, can it be?   10

MALEVOLE

Can?

PIETRO

Discovered he not Ferneze?

MALEVOLE

Yes, but why? but why? For love to thee?—Much, much!—
To be revenged upon his rival, who had thrust his jaws awry,
who being slain, supposed by thine own hands, defended by   15
his sword, made thee most loathsome, him most gracious
with thy loose princess; thou, closely yielding egress and
regress to her, madest him heir, whose hot unquiet lust
straight toused thy sheets, and now would seize thy state.
Politician! Wise man! Death, to be led to the stake like a bull 20
by the horns, to make even kindness cut a gentle throat!
Life, why art thou numbed? Thou foggy dullness, speak!
Lives not more faith in a home-thrusting tongue than in
these fencing tip-tap courtiers?

Enter CELSO *with a hermit's gown and beard*

PIETRO

Lord Malevole, if this be true—   25

MALEVOLE

If? Come, shade thee with this disguise. If? Thou shalt

17 *closely* secretly
19 *toused* rumpled
25 *Pietro* ed. (Celso Qq)

handle it; he shall thank thee for killing thyself. Come,
follow my directions, and thou shalt see strange sleights.

PIETRO
World, whither wilt thou?

MALEVOLE
Why, to the devil. Come, the morn grows late;   30
A steady quickness is the soul of state.   *Exeunt*

Act IV, Scene i

Enter MAQUERELLE *knocking at the ladies' door*

MAQUERELLE
Medam, medam, are you stirring medam? If you be stirring,
medam—if I thought I should disturb ye—

[*Enter* PAGE]

PAGE
My lady is up, forsooth.

MAQUERELLE
A pretty boy; faith, how old art thou?

PAGE
I think fourteen.   5

MAQUERELLE
Nay, and ye be in the 'teens—are ye a gentleman born? Do
you know me? My name is Medam Maquerelle; I lie in the
old Cunnycourt—

[PAGE]
See, here the ladies.

Enter BIANCA *and* EMILIA

BIANCA
A fair day to ye, Maquerelle.   10

EMILIA
Is the duchess up yet, sentinel?

MAQUERELLE
O ladies, the most abominable mischance! O dear ladies, the
most piteous disaster! Ferneze was taken last night in the
duchess' chamber. Alas! the duke catched him and killed
him.   15

---

31 *state* statecraft
 8 *Cunnycourt* rabbit-warren (Lat. cuniculus) bawdy

BIANCA

Was he found in bed?

MAQUERELLE

O no, but the villainous certainty is, the door was not bolted,
the tongue-tied hatch held his peace; so the naked truth is,
he was found in his shirt, whilst I, like an arrant beast, lay
in the outward chamber, heard nothing; and yet they came   20
by me in the dark, and yet I felt them not, like a senseless
creature as I was. O beauties, look to your busk-points—if
not chastely, yet charily. Be sure the door be bolted. Is your
lord gone to Florence?

BIANCA

Yes, Maquerelle.   25

MAQUERELLE

I hope you'll find the discretion to purchase a fresh gown
for his return. Now, by my troth, beauties, I would ha' ye
once wise: he loves you, pish! he is witty, bubble! fair-
proportioned, mew! nobly born, wind! Let this be still your
fixed position: esteem me every man according to his good   30
gifts, and so ye shall ever remain most dear, and most
worthy to be most dear ladies.

EMILIA

Is the duke returned from hunting yet?

MAQUERELLE

They say not yet.

BIANCA

'Tis now in midst of day.   35

EMILIA

How bears the duchess with this blemish now?

MAQUERELLE

Faith, boldly; strongly defies defame, as one that hath a duke
to her father. And there's a note to you: be sure of a stout
friend in a corner, that may always awe your husband. Mark
the 'haviour of the duchess now: she dares defame, cries   40
'Duke, do what thou canst, I'll quit mine honour'; nay, as
one confirmed in her own virtue against ten thousand
mouths that mutter her disgrace, she's presently for dances.

18 *hatch* half-door
22 *busk-points* the whalebone busk of stays was fastened to the
   front by lace points
29–32 *Let . . . ladies* See the Dedication to Sir Philip Sidney's
   Arcadia (1590); 'most deare, and most worthy to be most deare
   Lady'
41 *quit* requite, clear   43 *presently* immediately

Enter FERRARDO

BIANCA
For dances?

MAQUERELLE
Most true.   45

EMILIA
Most strange. See, here's my servant, young Ferrardo. How
many servants thinkest thou I have, Maquerelle?

MAQUERELLE
The more, the merrier: 'twas well said, use your servants as
you do your smocks, have many, use one, and change often,
for that's most sweet and courtlike.   50

FERRARDO
Save ye, fair ladies, is the duke returned?

BIANCA
Sweet sir, no voice of him as yet in court.

FERRARDO
'Tis very strange.

BIANCA
And how like you my servant, Maquerelle?

MAQUERELLE
I think he could hardly draw Ulysses' bow; but, by my   55
fidelity, were his nose narrower, his eyes broader, his hands
thinner, his lips thicker, his legs bigger, his feet lesser, his
hair blacker, and his teeth whiter, he were a tolerable sweet
youth, i' faith. And he will come to my chamber, I will read
him the fortune of his beard.   60

Cornets sound

FERRARDO
Not yet returned I fear; but the duchess approacheth.

Act IV, Scene ii

Enter MENDOZA *supporting* [AURELIA]: GUERRINO. *The ladies that
are on the stage rise.* FERRARDO *ushers in* AURELIA, *and then takes
a lady to tread a measure*

AURELIA
We will dance—music!—we will dance.

46 *servant* lover
54–60 *And how . . . beard* they are speaking about the page
s.d. *measure* dance

GUERRINO
'Les quanto', lady, 'Pensez bien', 'Passa regis', or 'Bianca's brawl'?

AURELIA
We have forgot the brawl.

FERRARDO
So soon? 'Tis wonder.   5

GUERRINO
Why, 'tis but two singles on the left, two on the right, three doubles forward, a traverse of six round; do this twice; three singles side, galliard trick of twenty, coranto-pace; a figure of eight, three singles broken down, come up, meet, two doubles, fall back, and then honour.   10

AURELIA
O Daedalus, thy maze! I have quite forgot it.

MAQUERELLE
Trust me, so have I, saving the falling back, and then honour.

Enter PREPASSO

AURELIA
Music, music!

PREPASSO
Who saw the duke? The duke?   15

Enter EQUATO

AURELIA
Music!

11 *Daedalus* Daedalus constructed the maze, or Cretan labyrinth, for Minos
15 *Equato* ed. (*Pre*: Q)

2-3 *'Les quanto'* . . . *brawl.* 'Les quanto' may be 'a courtlie daunce called *Les Guanto'*, cited by Bullen from A. Mundy, *Banquet of Daintie Conceits* (1588); 'Passa regis' is possibly a 'King's Jig' (Wood); and 'Bianca's brawl' is probably a provocative jest. The brawl (Fr. *branle*) was sometimes danced in a ring, sometimes 'at length'. Guerrino here begins a 'branle double'. A galliard was usually in triple time, its steps consisting of five movements of the feet ('cinquepace') and a characteristic leap, hence 'trick of twenty' may be an emphatic description of the 'sault'; 'coranto-pace' indicates a lively dance (Fr. *courante*); 'broken down' means 'singly'. Guerrino clearly leads the company into a disorganised climax. For an account of a great variety of French dances see Jehan Tabouret, anagrammatised into Thoinot Arbeau, *Orchésographie*, 1588-9; for the music hear 'Court Dances of Medieval France', from Arbeau's *Orchésographie*, Telemann Society recording, Mono TV 4008.

EQUATO

The duke? Is the duke returned?

AURELIA

Music!

Enter CELSO

CELSO

The duke is either invisible, or else is not.

AURELIA

We are not pleased with your intrusion upon our private   20
retirement. We are not pleased; you have forgot yourselves.

Enter a PAGE

CELSO

Boy, thy master? Where's the duke?

PAGE

Alas, I left him burying the earth with his spread joyless
limbs. He told me he was heavy, would sleep; bid me walk
off, for that the strength of fantasy oft made him talk in his   25
dreams. I straight obeyed, nor ever saw him since; but,
whereso'er he is, he's sad.

AURELIA

Music, sound high, as is our heart! Sound high!

Act IV, Scene iii

Enter MALEVOLE, *and* PIETRO *disguised like an hermit*

MALEVOLE

The duke—peace!—the duke is dead.

AURELIA

Music!

MALEVOLE

Is't music?

MENDOZA

Give proof.

FERRARDO

How?   5

CELSO

Where?

PREPASSO

When?

MALEVOLE

Rest in peace, as the duke does; quietly sit. For my own part,
I beheld him but dead, that's all. Marry, here's one can give
you a more particular account of him.   10

MENDOZA
  Speak, holy father, nor let any brow within this presence
  fright thee from the truth. Speak confidently and freely.
AURELIA
  We attend.
PIETRO
  Now had the mounting sun's all-ripening wings
  Swept the cold sweat of night from earth's dank breast,   15
  When I (whom men call Hermit of the Rock)
  Forsook my cell, and clambered up a cliff,
  Against whose base the heady Neptune dashed
  His high-curled brows; there 'twas I eased my limbs,
  When, lo! my entrails melted with the moan   20
  Someone, who far 'bove me was climbed, did make—
  I shall offend.
MENDOZA
  Not.
AURELIA
  On.
PIETRO
  Methinks I hear him yet—'O female faith!   25
  Go sow the ingrateful sand, and love a woman.
  And do I live to be the scoff of men,
  To be the wittol-cuckold, even to hug
  My poison! Thou knowest, O truth!
  Sooner hard steel will melt with southern wind,   30
  A seaman's whistle calm the ocean,
  A town on fire be extinct with tears,
  Than women, vowed to blushless impudence,
  With sweet behaviour and soft minioning,
  Will turn from that where appetite is fixed.   35
  O powerful blood, how thou dost slave their soul!
  I wash'd an Ethiop, who, for recompense
  Sullied my name. And must I then be forced
  To walk, to live thus black? Must? Must? Fie!
  He that can bear with "must", he cannot die'.   40
  With that he sighed so passionately deep
  That the dull air even groaned. At last, he cries,
  'Sink shame in seas, sink deep enough!', so dies.
  For then I viewed his body fall and souse
  Into the foamy main. O then I saw   45

41 *so* Q1 (too Q, Q2)
44 *souse* plunge heavily

That which methinks I see; it was the duke,
Whom straight the nicer-stomached sea belched up.
But then—

MALEVOLE
Then came I in; but 'las, all was too late,
For even straight he sunk.

PIETRO   Such was the duke's sad fate.   50

CELSO
A better fortune to our Duke Mendoza!

OMNES
Mendoza!

Cornets flourish

MENDOZA
A guard, a guard!

Enter a GUARD

We, full of hearty tears
For our good father's loss—
For so we well may call him   55
Who did beseech your loves for our succession—
Cannot so lightly over-jump his death
As leave his woes revengeless. (*To* AURELIA) Woman of
                                                    shame,
We banish thee for ever to the place
From whence this good man comes; nor permit,   60
On death, unto the body any ornament;
But base as was thy life, depart away.

AURELIA
Ungrateful—

MENDOZA
Away!

AURELIA
Villain, hear me.   65

PREPASSO and GUERRINO *lead away* [AURELIA]

MENDOZA
Begone! My lords,
Address to public council; 'tis most fit,
The train of Fortune is borne up by wit.
Away! Our presence shall be sudden; haste.

All depart saving MENDOZA, MALEVOLE *and* PIETRO

MALEVOLE
Now, you egregious devil; ha, ye murdering politician, how   70
dost, duke? How dost look now? Brave duke, i' faith!

67 *address to* prepare for

MENDOZA

How did you kill him?

MALEVOLE

Slatted his brains out, then soused him in the briny sea.

MENDOZA

Brained him and drowned him too?

MALEVOLE

O 'twas best, sure work. For, he that strikes a great man, let　75
him strike home, or else 'ware, he'll prove no man. Shoulder
not a huge fellow, unless you may be sure to lay him in the
kennel.

MENDOZA

A most sound brain-pan! I'll make you both emperors.

MALEVOLE

Make us Christians, make us Christians!　　　　　　　　80

MENDOZA

I'll hoist ye, ye shall mount.

MALEVOLE

To the gallows, say ye? Come: *Praemium incertum petit
certum scelus.* How stands the progress?

MENDOZA

Here, take my ring unto the citadel;
Have entrance to Maria, the grave duchess　　　　　　85
Of banished Altofront. Tell her we love her.
Omit no circumstance to grace our person. Do't.

MALEVOLE

I'll make an excellent pander. Duke, farewell; 'dieu, adieu,
duke.

MENDOZA

Take Maquerelle with thee, for 'tis found　　　　　　90
None cuts a diamond but a diamond.　　　*Exit* MALEVOLE
Hermit, thou art a man for me, my confessor;
O thou selected spirit, born for my good,
Sure thou wouldst make an excellent elder
In a deformed church—　　　　　　　　　　95
Come, we must be inward; thou and I all one.

---

73 *Slatted* knocked
78 *kennel* gutter
82–3 *Praemium . . . scelus* 'He seeks uncertain reward, certain guilt'
　　(based on 'praemium incertum petis Certum scelus', Seneca,
　　Phoenissae, ll. 632–3)
88–9 *'dieu . . . duke* grotesque Marstonian word-play
95 *deformed church* irregular, i.e. Puritan (Wine)
96 *inward* intimate

PIETRO
>I am glad I was ordained for ye.

MENDOZA
>Go to, then; thou must know that Malevole is a strange
>villain; dangerous, very dangerous; you see how broad 'a
>speaks, a gross-jawed rogue. I would have thee poison him.   100
>He's like a corn upon my great toe, I cannot go for him, he
>must be cored out; he must. Wilt do't, ha?

PIETRO
>Anything, anything.

MENDOZA
>Heart of my life! Thus, then. To the citadel;
>Thou shalt consort with this Malevole;   105
>There being at supper, poison him. It shall be laid
>Upon Maria, who yields love or dies.
>Scud quick like lightning!

PIETRO
>Good deeds crawl, but mischief flies.   *Exit* PIETRO

Enter MALEVOLE

MALEVOLE
>Your devilship's ring has no virtue. The buff-captain, the   110
>sallow Westphalian gammon-faced zaza cries, 'Stand out!';
>must have a stiffer warrant, or no pass into the castle of
>comfort.

MENDOZA
>Command our sudden letter. Not enter, sha't? What place is
>there in Genoa but thou shalt? Into my heart, into my very   115
>heart. Come, let's love—we must love, we two, soul and
>body.

MALEVOLE
>How didst like the hermit? A strange hermit, sirrah.

MENDOZA
>A dangerous fellow, very perilous. He must die.

MALEVOLE
>Ay, he must die.   120

 99 *broad* freely
110 *virtue* effect, referring to l. 84
     buff-captain leather-jerkined captain of the citadel
111 *Westphalian gammon-faced* pig-faced ('That Westphalian gamon
     Cloue-stuck face', *Scourge of Villanie*, VII, l. 115: Westphalian
     pigs produced good bacon)
     zaza possibly from 'huszar' (Hung.), military freebooter
114 *sha't?* shalt not?

MENDOZA
  Thou'st kill him. We are wise; we must be wise.
MALEVOLE
  And provident.
MENDOZA
  Yea, provident. Beware an hypocrite;
  A churchman once corrupted, O avoid!—
  A fellow that makes religion his stalking-horse,   125
  Shoots under his belly, he breeds a plague.
  Thou shalt poison him.
MALEVOLE
  Ho, 'tis wondrous necessary. How?
MENDOZA
  You both go jointly to the citadel;
  There sup, there poison him. And Maria,   130
  Because she is our opposite, shall bear
  The sad suspect, on which she dies, or loves us.
MALEVOLE
  I run.   *Exit* MALEVOLE
MENDOZA
  We that are great, our sole self-good still moves us.
  They shall die both, for their deserts crave more   135
  Than we can recompense; their presence still
  Imbraids our fortunes with beholdingness,
  Which we abhor; like deed, not doer. Then conclude,
  They live not to cry out ingratitude.
  One stick burns t'other, steel cuts steel alone: 140
  'Tis good trust few; but O, 'tis best trust none.
                                        Exit MENDOZA

121 *Thou'st* Thou must
126 *Shoots . . . belly* marginal in Q, Q2 (not in Q1)
131 *opposite* opponent
132 *sad suspect* heavy suspicion
137 *Imbraids* upbraids
     beholdingness indebtedness

125–6 *A fellow . . . plague.* Wood suggests that 'Shoots under his belly' is
   not a marginal addition but a stage direction, and that Mendoza 'goes
   through the motion of shooting under the belly of his horse'. The
   actor's direction seems unprofessionally vague; does he shoot under
   his own belly or Malevole's? The force of 'shoots' seems required to
   bring the mental context of 'breeds a plague' into adequate intelligibility.
   I have accommodated the words in the text where Marston seems most
   probably to have been intending they should be placed.

Act IV, Scene iv

Enter MALEVOLE *and* PIETRO, *still disguised, at several doors*

MALEVOLE
How do you? How dost, duke?

PIETRO
O, let the last day fall; drop, drop on our cursed heads! Let
heaven unclasp itself, vomit forth flames!

[handwritten: illusion that this is a fiction, a play)]
[handwritten: (cont. illusion — which breaks]

MALEVOLE
O, do not rant, do not turn player—there's more of them
than can well live one by another already. What, art an infidel   5
still?

PIETRO
I am amazed, struck in a swoon with wonder! I am commanded to poison thee.

MALEVOLE
I am commanded to poison thee, at supper.

PIETRO
At supper?   10

MALEVOLE
In the citadel.

PIETRO
In the citadel?

MALEVOLE
Cross-capers! Tricks! Truth o' heaven, he would discharge
us as boys do eldern guns, one pellet to strike out another.
Of what faith art now?   15

PIETRO
All is damnation, wickedness extreme; there is no faith in
man.

MALEVOLE
In none but usurers and brokers, they deceive no man; men
take 'em for bloodsuckers, and so they are. Now God
deliver me from my friends!   20

PIETRO
Thy friends?

MALEVOLE
Yes, from my friends; for from mine enemies I'll deliver
myself. O, cut-throat friendship is the rankest villainy!
Mark this Mendoza, mark him for a villain; but heaven will
send a plague upon him for a rogue.   25

4 *rant* ed. (rand Q2, Q; raue Q1)
14 *eldern guns* popguns of elder wood

PIETRO

O world!

MALEVOLE

World! 'Tis the only region of death, the greatest shop of
the devil, the cruelest prison of men, out of the which none
pass without paying their dearest breath for a fee. There's
nothing perfect in it but extreme, extreme calamity, such as 30
comes yonder.

Act IV, Scene v

Enter AURELIA, *two halberts before, and two after, supported by*
 CELSO *and* FERRARDO; AURELIA *in base mourning attire*

AURELIA

To banishment! Led on to banishment!

PIETRO

Lady, the blessedness of repentance to you.

AURELIA

Why? Why? I can desire nothing but death,
Nor deserve anything but hell.
If heaven should give sufficiency of grace 5
To clear my soul, it would make heaven graceless;
My sins would make the stock of mercy poor,
O, they would tire heaven's goodness to reclaim them:
Judgement is just, yet from that vast villain;
But sure, he shall not miss sad punishment 10
'Fore he shall rule. On to my cell of shame!

PIETRO

My cell 'tis, lady; where, instead of masques,
Music, tilts, tourneys, and such courtlike shows,
The hollow murmur of the checkless winds
Shall groan again, whilst the unquiet sea 15
Shakes the whole rock with foamy battery.
There, usherless, the air comes in and out;
The rheumy vault will force your eyes to weep,
Whilst you behold true desolation;

 30 *perfect* completed
s.d. *halberts* guards bearing halberds (combination of spear and
  battle-axe)
 8 *tire* Q, Q2 (try Q1)
 9 *yet* even though
 10 *sad* heavy
 17 *usherless* unannounced, without warning

A rocky barrenness shall pierce your eyes,   20
Where all at once one reaches where he stands,
With brows the roof, both walls with both his hands.

AURELIA

It is too good. Blessed spirit of my lord,
O, in what orb so'er thy soul is throned
Behold me worthily most miserable!   25
O, let the anguish of my contrite spirit
Entreat some reconciliation.
If not, O joy, triumph in my just grief!
Death is the end of woes, and tears' relief.

PIETRO

Belike your lord not loved you, was unkind.   30

AURELIA

O heaven!
As the soul loved the body, so loved he;
'Twas death to him to part my presence,
Heaven to see me pleased.
Yet I, like to a wretch given o'er to hell,   35
Brake all the sacred rites of marriage,
To clip a base, ungentle, faithless villain;
O God, a very pagan reprobate!—
What should I say? Ungrateful, throws me out,
For whom I lost soul, body, fame, and honour.   40
But 'tis most fit. Why should a better fate
Attend on any who forsake chaste sheets,
Fly the embrace of a devoted heart,
Joined by a solemn vow 'fore God and man,
To taste the brackish blood of beastly lust   45
In an adulterous touch? O ravenous immodesty,
Insatiate impudence of appetite!
Look, here's your end; for mark what sap in dust,
What sin in good, even so much love in lust.
Joy to thy ghost, sweet lord, pardon to me.   50

CELSO

'Tis the duke's pleasure this night you rest in court.

AURELIA

Soul, lurk in shades; run shame from brightsome skies,
In night the blind man misseth not his eyes.
                    Exit [with CELSO, FERRARDO *and halberts]*

45 *brackish* salty, licentious
46 *immodesty* excess
47 *impudence* shamelessness

JOHN MARSTON   [ACT IV

MALEVOLE

Do not weep, kind cuckold; take comfort, man; thy betters
have been beccos: Agamemnon, emperor of all the merry   55
Greeks, that tickled all the true Trojans, was a cornuto;
Prince Arthur, that cut off twelve kings' beards, was a
cornuto; Hercules, whose back bore up heaven, and got
forty wenches with child in one night—

PIETRO

Nay, 'twas fifty.   60

MALEVOLE

Faith, forty's enow, a' conscience—yet was a cornuto.
Patience; mischief grows proud; be wise.

PIETRO

Thou pinchest too deep, art too keen upon me.

MALEVOLE

Tut, a pitiful surgeon makes a dangerous sore; I'll tent thee
to the ground. Thinkest I'll sustain myself by flattering thee,   65
because thou art a prince? I had rather follow a drunkard,
and live by licking up his vomit, than by servile flattery.

PIETRO

Yet great men ha' done it.

MALEVOLE

Great slaves fear better than love, born naturally for a coal-
basket, though the common usher of princes' presence,   70
Fortune, hath blindly given them better place. I am vowed
to be thy affliction.

PIETRO

Prithee be; I love much misery, and be thou son to me.

MALEVOLE

Because you are an usurping duke—

Enter BILIOSO

(*To* BILIOSO) Your lordship's well returned from Florence.   75

64 *pitiful* full of pity
   tent clean out a lanced wound to prevent festering
69–70 *born . . . basket* for servile tasks

64–5 *Tut . . . ground.* Cf. *Il pastor fido*, III. v:

How much I grieue for thee: and if I haue
Piers't with my wordes thy soule, like a Phisicion I
Haue done, who searcheth first the wound
Where it suspected is: be quiet then
Good Nimph, and do not contradict that which
Is writ in heau'n aboue of thee. (Sig. L4v.)

BILIOSO

Well returned, I praise my horse.

MALEVOLE

What news from the Florentines?

BILIOSO

I will conceal the great duke's pleasure; only this was his
charge: his pleasure is, that his daughter die; Duke Pietro
be banished, for banishing his blood's dishonour; and that   80
Duke Altofront be re-accepted. This is all; but I hear Duke
Pietro is dead.

MALEVOLE

Ay, and Mendoza is duke; what will you do?

BILIOSO

Is Mendoza strongest?

MALEVOLE

Yet he is.   85

BILIOSO

Then yet I'll hold with him.

MALEVOLE

But if that Altofront should turn straight again?

BILIOSO

Why, then I would turn straight again.
'Tis good run still with him that hath most might;
I had rather stand with wrong, than fall with right.   90

MALEVOLE

What religion will you be of now?

BILIOSO

Of the duke's religion, when I know what it is.

MALEVOLE

O Hercules!

BILIOSO

Hercules? Hercules was the son of Jupiter and Alcmena.

MALEVOLE

Your lordship is a very witt-all.   95

BILIOSO

Wittol?

MALEVOLE

Ay, all-wit.

BILIOSO

Amphitryo was a cuckold.

MALEVOLE

Your lordship sweats; your young lady will get you a cloth

80 *banishing* proclaiming, a pun on 'ban'
98 *Amphitryo* Amphytryon was Alcmena's husband

for your old worship's brows.   *Exit* BILIOSO   100
Here's a fellow to be damned; this is his inviolable maxim,
'Flatter the greatest, and oppress the least'—a whoreson
flesh-fly, that still gnaws upon the lean, galled backs.

PIETRO

Why dost then salute him?

MALEVOLE

Faith, as bawds go to church, for fashion sake. Come, be   105
not confounded; thou art but in danger to lose a dukedom.
Think this:—this earth is the only grave and Golgotha
wherein all things that live must rot; 'tis but the draught
wherein the heavenly bodies discharge their corruption, the
very muckhill on which the sublunary orbs cast their excre-   110
ments. Man is the slime of this dung-pit, and princes are the
governors of these men; for, for our souls, they are as free as
emperors, all of one piece; there goes but a pair of shears
betwixt an emperor and the son of a bagpiper—only the
dyeing, dressing, pressing, glossing makes the difference.   115
Now, what art thou like to lose?
A jailor's office to keep men in bonds,
Whilst toil and treason all life's good confounds.

PIETRO

I here renounce for ever regency.
O Altofront, I wrong thee to supplant thy right,   120
To trip thy heels up with a devilish sleight,
For which I now from throne am thrown; world tricks
                                                  abjure,
For vengeance, though't comes slow, yet it comes sure.
O I am changed; for here, 'fore the dread power,
In true contrition I do dedicate   125
My breath to solitary holiness,
My lips to prayer; and my breast's care shall be
Restoring Altofront to regency.

MALEVOLE

Thy vows are heard, and we accept thy faith.
                          Undisguiseth himself

Enter FERNEZE *and* CELSO

108 *draught* privy
110 *sublunary* lying between the orbit of moon and earth
113–14 *there . . . bagpiper* they are cut out of the same cloth ('There
     went but a pair of shears between them', proverbial phrase)
115 *glossing* finishing
118 *confounds* destroys

Banish amazement. Come, we four must stand full shock of   130
Fortune; be not so wonder-stricken.

PIETRO

Doth Ferneze live?

FERNEZE

For your pardon.

PIETRO

Pardon and love. Give leave to recollect
My thoughts, dispersed in wild astonishment.   135
My vows stand fixed in heaven, and from hence
I crave all love and pardon.

MALEVOLE

Who doubts of providence
That sees this change? A hearty faith to all!
He needs must rise, who can no lower fall,   140
For still impetuous vicissitude
Touseth the world; then let no maze intrude
Upon your spirits. Wonder not I rise,
For who can sink, that close can temporise?
The time grows ripe for action; I'll detect   145
My privat'st plot, lest ignorance fear suspect.
Let's close to counsel, leave the rest to fate;
Mature discretion is the life of state.   *Exeunt*

Act V, Scene i

Enter BILIOSO *and* PASSARELLO

BILIOSO

Fool, how dost thou like my calf in a long stocking?

PASSARELLO

An excellent calf, my lord.

BILIOSO

This calf hath been a reveller this twenty year. When
Monsieur Gundi lay here ambassador, I could have carried
a lady up and down at arm's end in a platter; and I can tell   5
you, there were those at that time who, to try the strength
of a man's back and his arm, would be coistered. I have

140 *who* Q1, Q2 (not in Q)
142 *Touseth* Q, Q2 (Looseth Q1)
    maze amazement
145 *detect* reveal
147 *close* meet
  7 *coistered* curled up (probably nonce word, and bawdy)

measured calves with most of the palace, and they come
nothing near me; besides, I think there be not many armours
in the arsenal will fit me, especially for the headpiece. I'll tell   10
thee—

PASSARELLO

What, my lord?

BILIOSO

I can eat stewed broth as it comes seething off the fire; or a
custard as it comes reeking out of the oven; and I think there
are not many lords can do it. A good pomander—a little   15
decayed in the scent, but six grains of musk ground with
rose-water, and tempered with a little civet, shall fetch her
again presently.

PASSARELLO

O ay, as a bawd with aqua-vitae.

BILIOSO

And, what, dost thou rail upon the ladies as thou wert wont?   20

PASSARELLO

I were better roast a live cat, and might do it with more
safety. I am as secret to thieves as their painting. There's
Maquerelle, oldest bawd, and a perpetual beggar. Did you
never hear of her trick to be known in the city?

BILIOSO

Never.   25

PASSARELLO

Why, she gets all the picture-makers to draw her picture;
when they have done, she most courtly finds fault with them
one after another, and never fetcheth them. They, in revenge
of this, execute her in pictures as they do in Germany, and
hang her in their shops. By this means is she better known   30
to the stinkards than if she had been five times carted.

BILIOSO

'Fore God, an excellent policy.

PASSARELLO

Are there any revels tonight, my lord?

BILIOSO

Yes.

PASSARELLO

Good my lord, give me leave to break a fellow's pate that   35
hath abused me.

15 *pomander* perfume ball, carried or worn
17 *fetch* restore
31 *stinkards* mob
    carted convicted bawds were carted to Bridewell for whipping

BILIOSO
Whose pate?
PASSARELLO
Young Ferrardo, my lord.
BILIOSO
Take heed, he's very valiant; I have known him fight eight
quarrels in five days, believe it.   40
PASSARELLO
O, is he so great a quarreller? Why then, he's an arrant
coward.
BILIOSO
How prove you that?
PASSARELLO
Why thus. He that quarrels seeks to fight; and he that seeks
to fight, seeks to die; and he that seeks to die, seeks never to   45
fight more; and he that will quarrel and seeks means never
to answer a man more, I think he's a coward.
BILIOSO
Thou canst prove anything.
PASSARELLO
Anything but a rich knave, for I can flatter no man.
BILIOSO
Well, be not drunk, good fool; I shall see you anon in the   50
presence.   [Exeunt]

Enter MALEVOLE *and* MAQUERELLE, *at several doors opposite,*
singing

MALEVOLE
'The Dutchman for a drunkard,'
MAQUERELLE
'The Dane for golden locks,'
MALEVOLE
'The Irishman for usquebaugh,'
MAQUERELLE
'The Frenchman for the (   ).'   55
MALEVOLE
O, thou art a blessed creature! Had I a modest woman to
conceal, I would put her to thy custody; for no reasonable
creature would ever suspect her to be in thy company. Ha,
thou art a melodious Maquerelle, thou picture of a woman
and substance of a beast!   60

54 *usquebaugh* whiskey (or any spirits; 'aqua vitae', Ir. 'uisge
    bheatha')
55 (   ) obviously 'pox', but not necessarily either said or printed

Enter PASSARELLO

MAQUERELLE
O, fool, will ye be ready anon to go with me to the revels?
The hall will be so pestered anon.

PASSARELLO
Ay, as the country is with attorneys.

MALEVOLE
What hast thou there, fool?

PASSARELLO
Wine. I have learned to drink since I went with my lord   65
ambassador; I'll drink to the health of Madam Maquerelle.

MALEVOLE
Why, thou wast wont to rail upon her.

PASSARELLO
Ay, but since I borrowed money of her, I'll drink to her
health now, as gentlemen visit brokers, or as knights send
venison to the city, either to take up more money, or to pro-   70
cure longer forbearance.

MALEVOLE
Give me the bowl. I drink a health to Altofront, our deposed
duke.

PASSARELLO
I'll take it; so. Now I'll begin a health to Madam Maquerelle.

MALEVOLE
Pugh! I will not pledge her.   75

PASSARELLO
Why, I pledged your lord.

MALEVOLE
I care not.

PASSARELLO
Not pledge Madam Maquerelle? Why, then will I spew up
your lord again with this fool's finger.

MALEVOLE
Hold; I'll take it.   80

MAQUERELLE
Now thou hast drunk my health, fool, I am friends with thee.

PASSARELLO
Art? Art?
    'When Griffon saw the reconciled quean,
        Offering about his neck her arms to cast,

62 *pestered* crowded
70 *take up* borrow
71 *forbearance* credit
83 *Griffon* a hero in Ariosto's *Orlando Furioso*

He threw off sword and heart's malignant stream,   85
And lovely her below the loins embrac'd.'
Adieu, Madam Maquerelle.   *Exit* PASSARELLO

MALEVOLE
And how dost thou think o' this transformation of state now?

MAQUERELLE
Verily, very well; for we women always note, the falling of
the one is the rising of the other; some must be fat, some   90
must be lean; some must be fools, and some must be lords;
some must be knaves, and some must be officers; some must
be beggars, some must be knights; some must be cuckolds,
and some must be citizens. As for example, I have two
court dogs, the most fawning curs, the one called Watch,   95
th'other Catch; now I, like Lady Fortune, sometimes love
this dog, sometimes raise that dog, sometimes favour Watch,
most commonly fancy Catch. Now, that dog which I favour,
I feed; and he's so ravenous that what I give he never chaws
it, gulps it down whole, without any relish of what he has,   100
but with a greedy expectation of what he shall have. The
other dog now—

MALEVOLE
No more dog, sweet Maquerelle, no more dog. And what
hope hast thou of the Duchess Maria? Will she stoop to the
duke's lure; will she come, thinkest?   105

MAQUERELLE
Let me see; where's the sign now? Ha' ye e'er a calendar?
Where's the sign, trow you?

MALEVOLE
Sign! Why, is there any moment in that?

MAQUERELLE
O, believe me, a most secret power. Look ye, a Chaldean or
an Assyrian (I am sure 'twas a most sweet Jew) told me,   110
court any woman in the right sign, you shall not miss. But
you must take her in the right vein then; as, when the sign
is in Pisces, a fishmonger's wife is very sociable; in Cancer,
a precisian's wife is very flexible; in Capricorn, a merchant's

---

89–90 *the falling . . . other* Maquerelle, for bawdy purposes, reverses
     the proverbial phrasing 'The rising of one man is the falling of
     another' (Erasmus, *Adagia* II, 1055 C: *Bona nemini hora est, quin
     alcui sit mala*)
104 *stoop* swoop, descend
105 *lure* falconer's device for recalling hawks
     come Q1, Q2 (cowe Q)
106 *sign* astrological sign of the zodiac   114 *precisian's* puritan's

wife hardly holds out; in Libra, a lawyer's wife is very tract-   115
able, especially if her husband be at the term; only in
Scorpio 'tis very dangerous meddling. Has the duke sent any
jewel, any rich stones?

Enter CAPTAIN

MALEVOLE
Ay, I think those are the best signs to take a lady in—
By your favour, signior, I must discourse with the Lady   120
Maria, Altofront's duchess. I must enter for the duke.

CAPTAIN
She here shall give you interview. I received the guardian-
ship of this citadel from the good Altofront, and for his use
I'll keep it, till I am of no use.

MALEVOLE
Wilt thou? O heavens, that a Christian should be found in a   125
buff-jerkin! Captain Conscience, I love thee, Captain. We
attend.   *Exit* CAPTAIN
And what hope hast thou of this duchess' easiness?

MAQUERELLE
'Twill go hard. She was a cold creature ever; she hated
monkeys, fools, jesters, and gentlemen-ushers extremely.   130
She had the vile trick on't, not only to be truly modestly
honourable in her own conscience, but she would avoid the
least wanton carriage that might incur suspect; as God bless
me, she had almost brought bed-pressing out of fashion; I
could scarce get a fine for the lease of a lady's favour once in   135
a fortnight.

MALEVOLE
Now, in the name of immodesty, how many maidenheads
hast thou brought to the block?

MAQUERELLE
Let me see. Heaven forgive us our misdeeds!—Here's the
duchess.   140

Act V, Scene ii

Enter MARIA *and* CAPTAIN

MALEVOLE
God bless thee, lady.

MARIA
Out of thy company.

116 *term* law-court session
133 *carriage* behaviour
135 *fine* fee

MALEVOLE
We have brought thee tender of a husband.

MARIA
I hope I have one already.

MAQUERELLE
Nay, by mine honour, madam, as good ha' ne'er a husband   5
as a banished husband; he's in another world now. I'll tell
ye, lady, I have heard of a sect that maintained, when the
husband was asleep, the wife might lawfully entertain
another man, for then her husband was as dead; much more
when he is banished.   10

MARIA
Unhonest creature!

MAQUERELLE
Pish! Honesty is but an art to seem so. Pray ye, what's
honesty, what's constancy, but fables feigned, odd old fools'
chat, devised by jealous fools to wrong our liberty?

MALEVOLE
Molly, he that loves thee is a duke, Mendoza; he will main-   15
tain thee royally, love thee ardently, defend thee powerfully,
marry thee sumptuously, and keep thee in despite of
Rosicleer or Donzel del Phoebo. There's jewels; if thou wilt,
so; if not, so.

MARIA
Captain, for God's sake, save poor wretchedness   20
From tyranny of lustful insolence!
Enforce me in the deepest dungeon dwell
Rather than here; here round about is hell.
O my dear'st Altofront, where'er thou breathe,
Let my soul sink into the shades beneath,   25
Before I stain thine honour; this thou hast:
And long as I can die, I will live chaste.

MALEVOLE
'Gainst him that can enforce, how vain is strife!

MARIA
She that can be enforced has ne'er a knife.
She that through force her limbs with lust enrolls,   30

3 *tender* offer, on Mendoza's behalf
15 *Molly* (Mully Qq) familiar form of Maria, Mary: 'Molly' was
   possibly already a term for a prostitute
18 *Rosicleer Donzel del Phoebo* heroes in *The Mirror of Knighthood*,
   Spanish popular romance trans. 1583–1601
20 *sake* Q (loue Q1, Q2)
29 *She . . . knife* Lucrece afterwards stabbed herself

Wants Cleopatra's asps and Portia's coals.
God amend you.   *Exit with* CAPTAIN

MALEVOLE
Now, the fear of the devil for ever go with thee! Maquerelle,
I tell thee, I have found an honest woman. Faith, I perceive,
when all is done, there is of women, as of all other things,   35
some good, most bad; some saints, some sinners. For as
nowadays no courtier but has his mistress, no captain but
has his cockatrice, no cuckold but has his horns, and no fool
but has his feather, even so, no woman but has her weakness
and feather too, no sex but has his—I can hunt the letter   40
no farther. [*Aside*] O God, how loathsome this toying is to
me! That a duke should be forced to fool it! Well, *Stultorum
plena sunt omnia*; better play the fool lord than be the fool
lord.—Now, where's your sleights, Madam Maquerelle?

MAQUERELLE
Why, are ye ignorant that 'tis said a squeamish, affected   45
niceness is natural to women, and that the excuse of their
yielding is only (forsooth) the difficult obtaining? You must
put her to't; women are flax, and will fire in a moment.

MALEVOLE
Why, was the flax put into thy mouth, and yet thou—Thou
set fire? Thou inflame her?   50

MAQUERELLE
Marry, but I'll tell ye now, you were too hot.

MALEVOLE
The fitter to have inflamed the flaxwoman.

MAQUERELLE
You were too boisterous, spleeny; for indeed—

MALEVOLE
Go to, thou art a weak pandress; now I see,
Sooner earth's fire heaven itself shall waste,   55
Than all with heat can melt a mind that's chaste.
Go thou, the duke's lime-twig! I'll make the duke turn thee
out of thine office. What, not get one touch of hope, and had
her at such an advantage!

MAQUERELLE
Now, o' my conscience, now I think in my discretion, we   60

31 *Wants . . . coals* Cleopatra died of snake bites; Portia, wife of
    Brutus, swallowed fire
38 *cockatrice* whore
42-3 *Stultorum . . . omnia* 'All places are full of fools' (Cicero,
    Epistolae ad Familiares, ix. 22)
57 *lime-twig* twig smeared with bird-lime; snare for Maria

did not take her in the right sign; the blood was not in the
true vein, sure.   *Exit*

Enter BILIOSO

BILIOSO

Make way there! The duke returns for the enthronement.
Malevole—

MALEVOLE

Out, rogue!   65

BILIOSO

Malevole!

MALEVOLE

'Hence, ye gross-jawed peasantly—out, go!'

BILIOSO

Nay, sweet Malevole, since my return I hear you are become
the thing I always prophesied would be, an advanced virtue,
a worthily employed faithfulness, a man o' grace, dear   70
friend. Come; what? *Si quoties peccant homines.*—If as often
as courtiers play the knaves honest men should be angry—
why, look ye, we must collogue sometimes, forswear sometimes.

MALEVOLE

Be damned sometimes.   75

BILIOSO

Right. *Nemo omnibus horis sapit*; no man can be honest at all
hours. Necessity often depraves virtue.

MALEVOLE

I will commend thee to the duke.

BILIOSO

Do; let us be friends, man.

MALEVOLE

And knaves, man.   80

BILIOSO

Right; let us prosper and purchase; our lordships shall live
and our knavery be forgotten.

MALEVOLE

He that by any ways gets riches, his means never shames
him.

67 *'Hence . . . go!'* refers to II. iii, 30
71 *Si . . . homines* 'If as often as men sin' (Ovid, *Tristia* II, 33–4,
   'si, quotiens peccant homines, sua fulmina mittat/Iuppiter, exiguo
   tempore inermis erit'); Malevole completes the thought in his
   own terms   73 *collogue* pretend
76 *Nemo . . . sapit* Pliny, *Naturalis Historia*, Bk. VII, xli. 2
81 *purchase* acquire wealth

BILIOSO
>True.   85

MALEVOLE
>For impudency and faithlessness are the main stays to
>greatness.

BILIOSO
>By the Lord, thou art a profound lad.

MALEVOLE
>By the Lord, thou art a perfect knave. Out, ye ancient
>damnation!   90

BILIOSO
>Peace, peace! And thou wilt not be a friend to me as I am a
>knave, be not a knave to me as I am thy friend and disclose
>me. Peace! Cornets!

Act V, Scene iii

Enter PREPASSO *and* FERRARDO, *two* PAGES *with lights*, CELSO
and EQUATO, MENDOZA *in duke's robes, and* GUERRINO

MENDOZA
>On, on; leave us, leave us.
>>   *Exeunt all saving* MALEVOLE
>Stay, where is the hermit?

MALEVOLE
>With Duke Pietro, with Duke Pietro.

MENDOZA
>Is he dead? Is he poisoned?

MALEVOLE
>Dead, as the duke is.   5

MENDOZA
>Good, excellent. He will not blab; secureness lives in secrecy.
>Come hither, come hither.

1–17 *On . . . man.* After these opening lines Q has a repetitive scene
entrance:
>*Enter* MALEVOLE *and* MENDOZA
>MENDOZA
>>Hast been with Maria?
>MALEVOLE
>>As your scrivener to your usurer, I have dealt about taking of
>>this commodity; but she's cold-frosty.

If, as editors suggest, Marston intended to cancel the first eighteen
lines and recommence the scene with only Malevole and Mendoza, he
may have been prompted by stage economy; but he would soon realise
that Mendoza's decision to kill Maria would not find a place.

MALEVOLE

Thou hast a certain strong villainous scent about thee my
nature cannot endure.

MENDOZA

Scent, man? What returns Maria? What answer to our suit?   10

MALEVOLE

Cold, frosty; she is obstinate.

MENDOZA

Then she's but dead; 'tis resolute, she dies.

Black deed only through black deed safely flies.

MALEVOLE

Pugh! *Per scelera semper sceleribus tutum est iter.*

MENDOZA

What, art a scholar? Art a politician? Sure, thou art an arrant   15
knave.

MALEVOLE

Who, I? I ha' been twice an under-sheriff, man. Well, I will
go rail upon some great man, that I may purchase the
bastinado, or else go marry some rich Genoan lady, and
instantly go travel.   20

MENDOZA

Travel, when thou art married?

MALEVOLE

Ay, 'tis your young lord's fashion to do so, though he was so
lazy, being a bachelor, that he would never travel so far as
the university; yet when he married her, tails off, and Catso!
for England.   25

MENDOZA

And why for England?

MALEVOLE

Because there is no brothel-houses there.

MENDOZA

Nor courtesans?

MALEVOLE

Neither; your whore went down with the stews, and your
punk came up with your puritan.   30

MENDOZA

Canst thou empoison? Canst thou empoison?

14 *Per . . . iter* 'The safest way through crimes is always by crimes'
(Seneca, *Agamemnon* I, 115)
19 *bastinado* beating
24 *tails off* turns tail
30 *punk* whore; a common charge of hypocrisy

MALEVOLE

Excellently; no Jew, 'pothecary, or politician better. Look ye,
here's a box; whom wouldst thou empoison? Here's a box
[*Gives it*] which, opened and the fume taken up in conduits
thorough which the brain purges itself, doth instantly for   35
twelve hours' space bind up all show of life in a deep senseless sleep. Here's another [*Gives it*] which, being opened
under the sleeper's nose, chokes all the power of life, kills
him suddenly.

MENDOZA

I'll try experiments; 'tis good not to be deceived—so, so;   40
Catso!

Seems to poison MALEVOLE

Who would fear that may destroy?
Death hath no teeth or tongue;
And he that's great, to him are slaves
Shame, murder, fame, and wrong—   45
Celso!

Enter CELSO

CELSO

My honoured lord?

MENDOZA

The good Malevole, that plain-tongued man,
Alas, is dead on sudden, wondrous strangely.
He held in our esteem good place. Celso,   50
See him buried, see him buried.

CELSO

I shall observe ye.

MENDOZA

And Celso, prithee let it be thy care tonight
To have some pretty show, to solemnise
Our high instalment; some music, masquery.   55
We'll give fair entertain unto Maria,
The duchess to the banished Altofront.
Thou shalt conduct her from the citadel
Unto the palace; think on some masquery.

CELSO

Of what shape, sweet lord?   60

MENDOZA

What shape? Why, any quick-done fiction—
As some brave spirits of the Genoan dukes

34 *conduits* Q corrected (comodities Q uncorrected)
61 *What* ed. (Why Qq)

To come out of Elysium, forsooth,
Led in by Mercury, to gratulate
Our happy fortune—some such anything,   65
Some far-fet trick, good for ladies, some stale toy
Or other, no matter so't be of our devising.
Do thou prepar't, 'tis but for a fashion sake;
Fear not, it shall be graced man, it shall take.

CELSO
All service.   70

MENDOZA
All thanks; our hand shall not be close to thee. Farewell.
(*Aside*) Now is my treachery secure, nor can we fall;
Mischief that prospers men do virtue call.
I'll trust no man; he that by tricks gets wreaths,
Keeps them with steel; no man securely breathes   75
Out of deserved ranks; the crowd will mutter, 'fool';
Who cannot bear with spite, he cannot rule.
The chiefest secret for a man of state
Is, to live senseless of a strengthless hate.   *Exit* MENDOZA

MALEVOLE
(*Starts up and speaks*) Death of the damned thief! I'll make   80
one i' the masque; thou shalt ha' some brave spirits of the
antique dukes.

CELSO
My lord, what strange delusion?

MALEVOLE
Most happy, dear Celso; poisoned with an empty box! I'll
give thee all, anon. My lady comes to court; there is a whirl   85
of fate comes tumbling on; the castle's captain stands for me,
the people pray for me, and the great leader of the just
stands for me. Then courage, Celso—
For no disastrous chance can ever move him
That leaveth nothing but a God above him.   [*Exeunt*]   90

Enter PREPASSO *and* BILIOSO, *two* PAGES *before them*;
MAQUERELLE, BIANCA *and* EMILIA

BILIOSO
Make room there, room for the ladies! Why, gentlemen,

---

64 *gratulate* greet
66 *far-fet trick* clever device; also bawdy, 'far fet and dear bought
   is good for ladies'
71 *close* niggardly
74 *wreaths* crowns (Harrison)
79 *senseless* indifferent

will not ye suffer the ladies to be entered in the great
chamber! Why, gallants! And you, sir, to drop your torch
where the beauties must sit too!

PREPASSO
And there's a great fellow plays the knave; why dost not   95
strike him?

BILIOSO
Let him play the knave, o' God's name; think'st thou I have
no more wit than to strike a great fellow? The music! More
lights! Revelling-scaffolds! Do you hear? Let there be oaths
enow ready at the door; swear out the devil himself. Let's   100
leave the ladies, and go see if the lords be ready for them.

All save the ladies depart

MAQUERELLE
And by my troth, beauties, why do you not put you into the
fashion? This is a stale cut, you must come in fashion. Look
ye, you must be all felt, felt and feather, a felt upon your bare
hair. Look ye, these tiring things are justly out of request now.   105
And—do you hear?—you must wear falling-bands, you must
come into the falling fashion; there is such a deal o' pinning
these ruffs, when the fine clean fall is worth all. And again, if you
should chance to take a nap in the afternoon, your falling-
bands requires no poting-stick to recover his form; believe   110
me, no fashion to the falling, I say.

BIANCA
And is not Signior Sir Andrew a gallant fellow now?

MAQUERELLE
By my maidenhead, la, honour and he agree as well together
as a satin suit and woollen stockings.

EMILIA
But is not Marshall Make-room, my servant in reversion, a   115
proper gentleman?

MAQUERELLE
Yes, in reversion, as he had his office; as in truth he hath all
things in reversion. He has his mistress in reversion, his
clothes in reversion, his wit in reversion, and indeed is a

104 *felt* hat
105 *tiring things* head-dresses
106 *falling-bands* collars, falling flat from the neck, and replacing
     ruffs in fashion
110 *poting-stick* poking-stick, for setting pleats
112 *Sir Andrew* ed. St. Andrew Q, Q2 (S. Andrew Iaques Q1; possibly
     a deleted joke on James I's Scottish courtiers)
115 *reversion* succession

suitor to me for my dog in reversion. But, in good verity, la,   120
he is as proper a gentleman in reversion as—and indeed, as
fine a man as may be, having a red beard and a pair of warped
legs.

BIANCA
But, i' faith, I am most monstrously in love with Count
Quidlibet-in-Quodlibet; is he not a pretty, dapper, unidle   125
gallant?

MAQUERELLE
He is even one of the most busy-fingered lords; he will put
the beauties to the squeak most hideously.

                    [*Enter* BILIOSO]

BILIOSO
Room! Make a lane there! The duke is entering. Stand
handsomely for beauties' sake. Take up the ladies there. So;   130
cornets, cornets!

Act V, Scene iv

Enter PREPASSO, *joins to* BILIOSO; *two* PAGES *and lights,* FERRARDO,
MENDOZA; *at the other door two* PAGES *with lights, and the*
CAPTAIN *leading in* MARIA; *the* DUKE *meets* MARIA *and closeth*
with her. The rest fall back

MENDOZA
Madam, with gentle ear receive my suit;
A kingdom's safety should o'er-peise slight rites,
Marriage is merely nature's policy.
Then, since unless our royal beds be joined,
Danger and civil tumult frights the state,   5
Be wise as you are fair, give way to fate.

MARIA
What wouldst thou, thou affliction to our house?
Thou ever-devil, 'twas thou that banished'st
My truly noble lord.

MENDOZA
I?   10

122–3 *red ... legs* possibly referring to Jonson's description of
   Marston in *Poetaster*
122 *warped* (warpt Q1, Q2; wrapt Q)
125 *Quidlibet-in-Quodlibet* 'Who you will of What you will' (Cf.
   Justice Quodlibet in *The Dutch Courtesan*)
s.d. *DUKE* i.e. Mendoza
   2 *o'er-peise* outweigh

MARIA
Ay, by thy plots, by thy black stratagems.
Twelve moons have suffered change since I beheld
The lovèd presence of my dearest lord.
O thou far worse than death! He parts but soul
From a weak body; but thou, soul from soul   15
Dissever'st, that which God's own hand did knit.
Thou scant of honour, full of devilish wit!

MENDOZA
We'll check your too-intemperate lavishness; I can and will.

MARIA
What canst?

MENDOZA
Go to; in banishment thy husband dies.   20

MARIA
He ever is at home that's ever wise.

MENDOZA
You'st ne'er meet more; reason should love control.

MARIA
Not meet?
She that dear loves, her love's still in her soul.

MENDOZA
You are but a woman, lady; you must yield.   25

MARIA
O, save me, thou innated bashfulness;
Thou only ornament of woman's modesty!

MENDOZA
Modesty? Death, I'll torment thee!

MARIA
Do; urge all torments; all afflictions try;
I'll die, my lords, as long as I can die.   30

MENDOZA
Thou obstinate, thou shalt die! Captain,
That lady's life is forfeited to justice;
We have examined her, and we do find
She hath empoisonèd the reverend hermit.
Therefore, we command severest custody.   35
Nay, if you'll do's no good,
You'st do's no harm; a tyrant's peace is blood.

MARIA
O thou art merciful! O gracious devil,

22 *You'st* You must
26 *innated* innate
32 *forfeited* Q1, Q2 (fortified Q)

Rather by much let me condemnèd be
For seeming murder than be damned for thee!   40
I'll mourn no more; come, girt my brows with flowers;
Revel and dance, soul, now thy wish thou hast;
Die like a bride, poor heart; thou shalt die chaste.

Enter AURELIA *in mourning habit*

AURELIA
'Life is a frost of cold felicity,
And death the thaw of all our vanity'—   45
Was't not an honest priest that wrote so?
MENDOZA
Who let her in?
BILIOSO
                    Forbear.
PREPASSO
                    Forbear.
AURELIA
Alas, calamity is everywhere;
Sad misery, despite your double doors,
Will enter even in court.   50
BILIOSO
Peace!
AURELIA
I ha' done. One word—take heed! I ha' done.

Enter MERCURY *with loud music*

MERCURY
Cyllenian Mercury, the god of ghosts,
From gloomy shades that spread the lower coasts,
Calls four high-famed Genoan dukes to come   55
And make this presence their Elysium;
To pass away this high triumphal night
With song and dances, court's more soft delight.
AURELIA
Are you god of ghosts? I have a suit depending in hell
betwixt me and my conscience; I would fain have thee help   60
me to an advocate.

44–5 *'Life . . . vanity'* Thomas Bastard, *Chrestoleros*, iv, 32 (1598);
    Bastard was vicar of Bere Regis
53 *Cyllenian Mercury* Mercury's birthplace was Mount Cyllene
54 *coasts* regions
59 *depending* pending

BILIOSO
Mercury shall be your lawyer, lady.

AURELIA
Nay faith, Mercury has too good a face to be a right lawyer.

PREPASSO
Peace, forbear! Mercury presents the masque.

*Cornets: the song to the cornets; which playing, the masque
enters:* MALEVOLE, PIETRO, FERNEZE, *and* CELSO *in white robes,
with dukes' crowns upon laurel-wreaths, pistolets and short
swords under their robes*

MENDOZA
Celso, Celso, court Maria for our love. Lady, be gracious, yet   65
grace—

MARIA
With me, sir?

MALEVOLE *takes his wife to dance*

MALEVOLE   Yes, more loved than our breath,
With you I'll dance.

MARIA   Why, then you dance with death.
But come sir, I was ne'er more apt to mirth.
Death gives eternity a glorious breath;   70
O, to die honoured, who would fear to die!

MALEVOLE
They die in fear who live in villainy.

MENDOZA
Yes, believe him, lady, and be ruled by him.

PIETRO
Madam, with me?

PIETRO *takes his wife* AURELIA *to dance*

AURELIA
                          Wouldst then be miserable?

PIETRO
I need not wish.   75

AURELIA
O, yet forbear my hand; away, fly, fly!
O seek not her that only seeks to die!

PIETRO
Poor loved soul!

62 *Mercury . . . lady* Mercury is patron of lawyers
65 *Celso* Mendoza mistakes the disguised Malevole
   court Q1, Q2 (count Q)

AURELIA

What, wouldst court misery?

PIETRO

Yes.

AURELIA

She'll come too soon. O my grieved heart!

PIETRO

Lady, ha' done, ha' done.   80
Come, let's dance; be once from sorrow free.

AURELIA

Art a sad man?

PIETRO   Yes, sweet.

AURELIA   Then we'll agree.

FERNEZE *takes* MAQUERELLE; *and* CELSO, BIANCA: *then the*
cornets sound the measure; one change and rest

FERNEZE

(*To* BIANCA) Believe it, lady; shall I swear?
Let me enjoy you in private and I'll marry you, by my soul.

BIANCA

I had rather you would swear by your body; I think that   85
would prove the more regarded oath with you.

FERNEZE

I'll swear by them both to please you.

BIANCA

O, damn them not both to please me, for God's sake.

FERNEZE

Faith, sweet creature, let me enjoy you tonight, and I'll
marry you tomorrow-fortnight, by my troth, la.   90

MAQUERELLE

On his troth, la! Believe him not; that kind of cony-
catching is as stale as Sir Oliver Anchovy's perfumed jerkin.
Promise of matrimony by a young gallant to bring a virgin
lady into a fool's paradise, make her a great woman, and then
cast her off—'tis as common, as natural to a courtier, as   95
jealousy to a citizen, gluttony to a puritan, wisdom to an
alderman, pride to a tailor, or an empty handbasket to one
of those sixpenny damnations. Of his troth, la! Believe him
not; traps to catch polecats!

91–2 *cony-catching* deceiving (card-sharping term)
92 *perfumed* jerkins were sometimes rubbed with oil
98 *sixpenny damnations* cheap whores
99 *polecats* whores

MALEVOLE
(*To* MARIA) Keep your face constant; let no sudden passion   100
Speak in your eyes.

MARIA
O my Altofront!

PIETRO
          [*To* AURELIA] A tyrant's jealousies
Are very nimble; you receive it all.

AURELIA
My heart, though not my knees, doth humbly fall
Low as the earth to thee.   105

PIETRO
Peace. Next change. [*To* MARIA] No words.

MARIA
Speech to such? Ay, O what will affords!

Cornets sound the measure over again: which danced,
they unmask

MENDOZA
Malevole!

They environ MENDOZA, *bending their pistols on him*

MALEVOLE
No.

MENDOZA
Altofront! Duke Pietro! Ferneze! Ha!   110

ALL
Duke Altofront! Duke Altofront!

Cornets, a flourish

MENDOZA
Are we surpris'd? What strange delusions mock
Our senses? Do I dream? Or have I dreamt
This two days' space? Where am I?

They seize upon MENDOZA

MALEVOLE
Where an arch-villain is.   115

MENDOZA
O lend me breath till I am fit to die;
For peace with heaven, for your own souls' sake,
Vouchsafe me life.

103 *receive* suffer, and understand
116 *breath till* Q, Q2 (breath to liue till Q1)

PIETRO

Ignoble villain, whom neither heaven nor hell,
Goodness of God or man, could once make good.   120

MALEVOLE

Base, treacherous wretch, what grace canst thou expect,
That hast grown impudent in gracelessness?

MENDOZA

O life!

MALEVOLE

Slave, take thy life.
Wert thou defenced, through blood and wounds,   125
The sternest horror of a civil fight,
Would I achieve thee; but prostrate at my feet,
I scorn to hurt thee. 'Tis the heart of slaves
That deigns to triumph over peasants' graves;
For such thou art, since birth doth ne'er enroll   130
A man 'mong monarchs, but a glorious soul.
O, I have seen strange accidents of state!—
The flatterer like the ivy clip the oak,
And waste it to the heart; lust so confirmed
That the black act of sin itself not shamed   135
To be termed courtship.
O they that are as great as be their sins,
Let them remember that th'inconstant people
Love many princes merely for their faces
And outward shows; and they do covet more   140
To have a sight of these than of their virtues.
Yet thus much let the great ones still conceive,
When they observe not heaven's imposed conditions,
They are no kings, but forfeit their commissions.

MAQUERELLE

O good my lord, I have lived in the court this twenty year;   145
they that have been old courtiers and come to live in the
city, they are spited at and thrust to the wall like apricocks,
good my lord.

BILIOSO

My lord, I did know your lordship in this disguise; you
heard me ever say if Altofront did return I would stand for   150

127 *achieve* make an end of
139 *princes* Wine (princes Q uncorrected; men Q corrected)
142 *conceive* ed. (conceale Q)
144 *kings* Wine (kings Q uncorrected; men Q corrected)

133–4 *The flatterer . . . heart.* A commonplace from Plutarch.

him; besides, 'twas your lordship's pleasure to call me wittol
and cuckold; you must not think, but that I knew you, I
would have put it up so patiently.

MALEVOLE

(*To* PIETRO *and* AURELIA) You o'er-joyed spirits, wipe your
           long wet eyes;
Hence with this man (*Kicks out* MENDOZA); an eagle takes not
             flies. 155
(*To* PIETRO *and* AURELIA) You to your vows; and thou unto
       the suburbs. (*To* MAQUERELLE)
(*To* BILIOSO) You to my worst friend I would hardly give;
Thou art a perfect old knave. (*To* CELSO *and the* CAPTAIN)
           All-pleased, live
You two unto my breast; (*To* MARIA) thou to my heart.
The rest of idle actors idly part. 160
And as for me, I here assume my right,
To which I hope all's pleased: to all, goodnight.

    Cornets, a flourish.

         Exeunt omnes

   F I N I S

Epilogus

Your modest silence, full of heedy stillness,
Makes me thus speak: a voluntary illness
Is merely senseless; but unwilling error,
Such as proceeds from too rash youthful fervour,
May well be called a fault, but not a sin; 5
Rivers take names from founts where they begin.
Then let not too severe an eye peruse
The slighter brakes of our reformed Muse,
Who could herself her self of faults detect,
But that she knows 'tis easy to correct, 10

153 *put it up* put up with it
154 *o'er-joyed* Q, Q2 (are ioyd Q1)
155 *an . . . flies* (Erasmus, *Adagia* II, 761 E, *Aquila non captat muscas*:
 Pettie-Young, *Civile Conversation*, I 200, 'the Eagle catcheth
 not flies')
156 *suburbs* brothels were situated in the suburbs
160 *The . . . part.* Q, Q2 (not in Q1)
 2 *illness* fault
 3 *merely* wholly
 8 *brakes* errors

Though some men's labour; troth, to err is fit,
As long as wisdom's not professed, but wit.
Then till another's happier Muse appears,
Till his Thalia feast your learned ears
To whose desertful lamps pleased Fates impart   15
Art above Nature, Judgment above Art,
   Receive this piece, which hope nor fear yet daunteth;
   He that knows most, knows most how much he wanteth.

F I N I S

14 *Thalia* the Muse of Comedy

DRAMABOOKS

WHEN ORDERING, please use the Standard Book Number consisting of the publisher's prefix, 8090–, plus the five digits following each title. (Note that the numbers given in this list are for paperback editions only. Many of the books are also available in cloth.)